For Lo... (handwritten)

THE HOUSE WITH 46 CHIMNEYS

KEN LUSSEY

Happy reading! (handwritten)

Ken Lussey (signature)

ARACHNID
PRESS

First published in Great Britain in 2020 by
Arachnid Press Ltd
91 Columbia Avenue
Livingston EH54 6PT
Scotland

www.arachnid.scot

ISBN: 978-1-8382530-1-1

Cover design by Carolyn Henry
Cover photographs by Maureen Lussey
The cover photographs are of Dunmore Park
Printed and bound in Great Britain by Inky Little Fingers Ltd,
Unit 3, Churcham Business Park, Churcham, Gloucester, GL2 8AX.

For my grandson Alistair,
who helped me write this book.

CHAPTER ONE

FRIDAY THE 8TH OF APRIL 1887

Ruby Simmonds took a last look round the kitchen. She didn't want to have to face cook's anger in the morning because she'd forgotten anything important. She especially didn't want Rose getting into trouble because of something that wasn't her fault.

Being twins had advantages. It meant you were never lonely and Ruby thought that some of the other girls, especially some of the older ones, were sometimes very lonely. But it did mean that people often saw you as interchangeable. They would sometimes blame one sister for something the other had done.

Rose would be the first up next morning, just as Ruby was the last to bed tonight. She'd be awakened before 6 o'clock by a knock on their door by the junior footman. He was entrusted with the servants' only alarm clock and had a list of who had to be woken up and when. Rose would then have to come down to clean and light the fires in the range and at the end of the kitchen. After that, she'd fill the coal buckets and make sure everything was ready for the house to start to come to life.

That meant, of course, that Ruby would also be awake early. She shared a narrow bed with Rose. Most of the female servants shared rooms. But Ruby and Rose were just 'wee slips of girls', in the housekeeper's words. As a result, they ıd the smallest room on the top floor of the rear part of the house and had to sleep in the same bed. At least once Rose was up, Ruby would have the bed to herself and be able to go back to sleep for a while.

Now they had turned 14, Ruby and Rose had asked Mama if they could have a bigger room and separate beds. While the lady's maid had an important position in the household, Mama still thought she needed to wait for the right moment to raise the subject with the housekeeper. Her word was law as far as the female servants were concerned. So far, the 'right moment' seemed not to have arrived.

Satisfied that she'd done everything that was needed, Ruby turned down the wicks in the two oil lamps that were still burning in the kitchen until the light died in each. Now she only had a single candle to light the way back to her room.

Ruby stopped to look out of a window into the courtyard. She'd noticed when outside for a few minutes earlier that there was a full moon in a clear sky. From the window she could see the dark shadows in the courtyard cast by the moonlight but couldn't see the moon itself. She turned and left the kitchen. As she moved out into it, the kitchen corridor felt cold.

The narrow stone staircase turned back on itself repeatedly as it led all the way up from the basement level of the rear range of the house, where the kitchen was, to the attic. As she climbed, her candle flickered, as if caught in a draught. She paused for a moment, to give it a chance to steady itself. Then she carried on up to the top of the stairs.

Ruby stepped out into the corridor that gave access to most of the female servants' rooms and then stopped. She'd been cold downstairs but here she suddenly felt chilled to the bone, as if she'd been standing in an icehouse.

The candle flickered, as the flame again seemed to respond

to movement in the air that she couldn't feel. Then it went out. She wasn't too worried. There was a little moonlight coming in through the window at the far end of the corridor. Enough to find her way back to their room and to Rose.

In the near darkness she became aware of a figure, a girl, hurrying down the corridor towards her. She wasn't sure how she saw enough detail to know it was Rose. Only the girl seemed a little older and was wearing old-fashioned clothes. Then she realised it wasn't Rose, for at that moment her sister emerged from their room carrying a candle, beyond the girl. Ruby could see Rose looking towards the two of them. Her sister's hand was held over her mouth and she had a look of horror on her face.

It all seemed to happen in an instant but Ruby still had time to realise that the girl was very frightened. The figure looked over her shoulder. Not towards Rose, who was still standing in the doorway of their room, but over her other shoulder, as if looking at someone Ruby couldn't see who was following her.

Then the girl cried out, 'Somebody please help me!' and broke into a run.

By now she had reached Ruby, who took a step backwards as the figure passed partly by her and partly, it felt, through her, intensifying the chill she had been feeling into something truly deep and terrifying.

In response, Ruby took another step backwards. She had forgotten she was standing at the top of the stone staircase. The second step she took was enough to cause most of her rear foot to go beyond the edge of the top step. She tumbled down the stairs, letting out a single scream as she fell.

When asked later, the other servants with rooms on the corridor said that Ruby's scream was the first noise they heard, though Rose's immediately followed it. The plea for help by the figure had been heard only by Ruby and by Rose.

Rose was the first to reach Ruby, who had come to rest some way down the staircase. One look at the angle of her sister's head was enough for Rose to know that Ruby was dead. Rose refused to leave Ruby's body until their mother had been fetched from her quarters elsewhere in the house.

CHAPTER TWO

WEDNESDAY THE 1ST OF APRIL 2020

The motorway was quiet as they joined it at the junction near Philpstoun. Kaleb was sitting behind his father, who had said little since they'd left home. Mummy and Daddy had argued again that morning, upstairs in their room, where they thought that the children couldn't hear them.

They'd been arguing a lot recently. Since the children had stopped going to school just under two weeks earlier, things had been difficult at home. Schools across Scotland had officially closed on the Friday, but many children at both their schools had been kept away by parents on the Thursday. On hearing this, Daddy had said the children should stay at home on the last day. Except for short breaks for walks in the village, they'd been at home ever since.

That's when the arguments had started. The following week, Edinburgh Council had opened schools, though not theirs, for children of key workers. Mummy was a detective inspector with Police Scotland and Daddy was a consultant surgeon at the Edinburgh Royal Infirmary. They certainly qualified as key workers. But while Mummy thought the children would be best going to the nearest open school each day, until the Easter holidays anyway, Daddy didn't believe that would be safe for the family.

Since then the children had spent some days at home on their own, and others with either Mummy or Daddy at home looking after them, though rarely both at the same time. Over this last weekend, Daddy had said that with the work he was now doing, there was just too much chance of catching coronavirus and passing it on to the children. Mummy had argued that it seemed to have little effect on children so they should stay together. In the end she had agreed with him. Kaleb knew that she hadn't been happy about it, though.

'Are you all right, Daddy?'

Kaleb was brought back to the present and to the car with a start as his sister Quoia, sitting in the front passenger seat, spoke.

'I'm fine, love. Just a little sad that it's come to this.'

'I'm a teenager now. I'd have had no problem looking after Jude and Kaleb at home.'

'I know that, Quoia. But as you've seen this last week, Mummy and I are both at work a lot of the time, even more than normal. Finding somewhere safer for the three of you will be a weight off both our minds. We agree that this is the best thing to do. That it's the least bad thing to do, anyway.'

'Why were you arguing again this morning, then? Mummy doesn't like Aunt Felicity, does she?'

'No, you're right, they've never got on. Felicity's ten years older than me and pretty much cut herself off from our parents when she went to university. She went through a wild phase when she was younger but settled down when she met and married your Uncle James, who was an architect. He designed the house she lives in. I keep in touch, of course. She is my sister after all.'

Daddy paused before continuing. 'Even when Felicity was working as an art teacher at a school in Stirling, she had an unusual approach to life. Your mother once described her as the "last hippy in Scotland" and the two of them have totally different views of the world. I suspect that working full time as an artist has allowed her even more scope to live exactly as she pleases.'

'Is that why we've seen so little of her, even though she lives not far away?' asked Quoia. 'The three of us haven't seen her since we called in on the way back from you taking us to Stirling Castle last autumn. When did you and Mummy last see her together?'

'It was probably at your Uncle James's funeral, which was three years ago. Look, the reason we were arguing this morning was that your mother doesn't think Felicity is the right sort of person to look after the three of you. But I've spoken to Felicity a lot about this over the past few days. She's promised not to do anything that puts the three of you at risk from the virus. She's also promised not to do anything that might be a bad influence on you. She says she's been strictly following the isolation rules and is really looking forward to having the three of you for company. I think she has ambitions to turn you into young artists while you're there.'

'But Mummy's still unhappy that we're going?' asked Quoia.

'She's unhappy that you'll be living away from us. I am too, of course. I think she just wishes that things were different, or at least that we had another option.'

Kaleb adjusted his glasses and saw Jude, sitting on the other side of the back seat, lean forward to speak. 'You said that Aunt Felicity's been following the isolation rules. We're not though, are we? What we're doing now, moving from where we live to somewhere further out into the country, isn't allowed, is it Daddy?'

Jude was two years older than Kaleb and just a year

younger than Quoia. Both Jude and Quoia took after their mother, with dark hair. Quoia's was long and straight, like their mother's. Kaleb sometimes felt like the odd one out. He had his father's blond hair and hoped he would share his father's height. He was already almost as tall as Jude, despite the difference in age. He knew Jude hated the idea that Kaleb might overtake him.

'No, I'm afraid you're right, Jude,' said their father. 'But sometimes you find yourself in a position where there's no right thing to do, yet you still have to do something. This just seems the best we can do in a bad situation.'

'But isn't there a risk that by taking the three of us into her house, Aunt Felicity could expose herself to the virus? Isn't that dangerous?' asked Jude.

'Your aunt's only too aware of that. But smoking apart, she has no underlying health issues and that's a chance she's happy to take for the sake of the three of you.'

'I didn't know she was a smoker!' said Quoia. 'That's gross!'

'I'm not sure she is now but she used to be,' said their father. 'I've never smelled smoke when I've visited. I'm sure you'll find she's a very considerate host, if a little scatter-brained and eccentric sometimes.'

'What about our cousins, Michael and Belinda?' asked Quoia. 'What if they want to come home?'

'I don't think that's likely. I think they'd already left university before your Aunt Felicity and Uncle James moved into the house, which was only a few months before your uncle suddenly died. As I said, that was three years ago. Felicity and James lived in Stirling before that. Belinda's an army officer based in southern England and Felicity says she's fully occupied right now, with no leave allowed during the emergency. Michael's been living in Canada for a couple of years. Felicity said he decided to stay there when the lockdowns started to happen. He'd not be able to get back now, even if he wanted to.'

*

They passed Grangemouth and its refinery and then the giant Kelpie horse sculptures standing right next to the motorway. Kaleb thought they looked far nicer than the flare and the storage tanks of the refinery. Not far beyond, their father took the junction signposted for the Kincardine and Clackmannanshire bridges. Then they drove through a village that he said was called Airth.

It was only a short time later that they turned right onto a minor road lined by hedges and grass. Standing a little back on both sides were large houses set in generally large gardens. Kaleb remembered this place from their visit the previous year. A couple of hundred metres further and the road split to pass both sides of a rectangular village green. Here there were some children's swings and a small roundabout, though there were no children playing on them. There was also a small open-sided structure that housed a drinking fountain and, beyond all that, a bowling green. Either side of the village green and overlooking its near end were rows of stone houses and cottages.

'Dunmore is very pretty,' said Quoia, 'especially in the sunshine like today. But there really isn't very much to do here. I don't think there's even a shop.'

'That's no bad thing,' said their father. 'I want you each to promise me that you'll remember why you're here, that you'll do what your aunt tells you to do, and that you'll remember the importance of social distancing and take no chances. Do you promise, Sequoia?'

Kaleb knew their father was being serious when he used Quoia's full name.

'Yes, of course.'

'And you Jude?'

'Yes, Daddy, you know I will.'

'What about you, Kaleb? You've been very quiet since we left home.'

'Yes, Daddy, I promise.'

'Good. You've all got plenty of ways to keep in touch. Mummy and I will try to talk to you on Skype every day. If you run into any issues or if I've misjudged my sister, ring me or, perhaps better, send me a text. Give me a chance to sort any problems out before you worry your mother with them.'

They'd turned left at the far end of the green, in front of a wooden building with a sign that said it was Dunmore Bowling Club. They then followed a narrow lane that ran past some houses on their right, before turning to run close to and parallel with the bank of a broad river.

'I looked on a map,' said Kaleb. 'That's the River Forth.'

'It is,' said their father. 'And even though you can all swim, it's somewhere to keep well clear of. It's tidal all the way up to Stirling and by the looks of it, the banks can get very muddy at low tide. Look, we're here.'

Not far along the length of road running alongside the shore, and beyond a hedge stretching back into the farmer's field on the left, stood Aunt Felicity's house. It looked out over the lane and across the river. Kaleb had loved it when they'd visited the previous year. Ever since the possibility had been mentioned, he'd been secretly looking forward to living here.

Their own house in Kirkliston was nice. It stood in its own garden and had a separate garage. It also had five bedrooms. That meant the children had one each, and there was a spare bedroom that Mummy and Daddy used for storing stuff they'd not got round to putting away anywhere else. But it looked much the same as all the other houses on their road, and on nearby roads, and the houses they were still building not far away on the edge of the village.

Aunt Felicity's house looked like nothing else nearby. Certainly, nothing else in Dunmore. When they'd last visited, Kaleb had left thinking that he wanted to be an architect like his uncle, who was someone he didn't have very clear memories of.

On first sight the house was as exciting as he remembered. It was two storeys high, like theirs in Kirkliston, but there was not much else in common between them. The front of its near end had a dark grey covering on the lower floor, round the front door and a single window, while the upper floor of this end was shaped as a gable and nearly the whole side facing the river was glass.

The rest of the house was set back a little from its near end. The ground floor was finished in white, while the upper floor again had huge windows looking out over the river. There was a balcony across much of the upper floor which was fronted by glass panels.

Beyond the house, separated by a slight gap and set back so it was barely visible at first, was a double garage finished in white. This had a glass walled gable on its upper floor, very like the one at the near end of the house. There was a lawn at the front, separated from the lane by a stone wall.

Daddy pulled onto the drive and parked next to a large blue car. Kaleb knew it was a 4x4, but cars weren't amongst the things that he loved, so he didn't take too much notice of them.

Daddy's car was a black Mercedes estate. Kaleb knew that because his father had been proud of his new car when he'd got it the previous autumn and Kaleb had sometimes helped him wash it on their drive. And Mummy's red Ford, of course.

As Kaleb walked round the back of the car, he saw Aunt Felicity approaching from the front door with a broad smile on her face. She was a little shorter than Daddy, but that would still have made her taller than Mummy. She had on jeans and a jumper with brightly coloured horizontal stripes. Kaleb always thought of Daddy as old, so if his aunt was ten years older, she had to be really old. She didn't look it. She had hair that was blonde and pulled back behind her head in a ponytail.

Quoia and Jude were closer, and their aunt gathered them up with both arms in a hug.

'Hello, welcome to Forthview House! I'm so pleased to see you all. I rattle round in this place and some company will be really welcome. I'm sure we'll all have a lovely time.'

His aunt saw Kaleb and released his brother and sister so she could hug him too.

Then she looked past Kaleb. 'Hello Henry. You're looking well. I suppose I'm not meant to hug you, am I?'

His father smiled. 'I'm sure that you're right, Fliss, but there's no way I'm not going to let these three go without a hug, so you and I might as well.'

Kaleb was shocked to see tears in his father's eyes. He'd never seen him cry before.

After they'd hugged, Aunt Felicity turned back towards the door. 'Do you want a cup of tea before you head back, Henry?'

'No thanks Fliss. I'm needed at the hospital later this

afternoon and Anna will already be on shift. As soon as we've emptied the car, I'll be on my way back. Anna sends her love, by the way.'

Felicity smiled again. 'I'm sure she does, Henry. Tell her that I'll be thinking of you both and that I'll take good care of these three so there's nothing for her to worry about.'

'I'll tell her.'

CHAPTER THREE

It had taken the five of them a little while to empty the car which, despite the size of its luggage area, had been full. As no-one had any idea how long the three children would be staying, Mummy and Daddy had packed everything they could possibly need for a long visit. There were bags of clothes and boxes of books, schoolwork and toys. Then there were laptops for Quoia and Jude, and Kaleb's iPad, as well as their consoles and a television.

Mummy and Daddy had also packed as much food and other household essentials as they could. It had been awkward to prepare for the stay because the supermarkets were limiting sales of most products to three items each and some things, like toilet rolls and flour, were extremely hard to find. Mummy and Daddy had made several individual trips to the Tesco in Queensferry and the supermarkets in Livingston, the town where Mummy worked.

Jude had asked whether they ought to be hoarding but was persuaded by Mummy that this was necessary to make sure Aunt Felicity could cope with the children's arrival. Fortunately, their aunt had said she had plenty of towels and bedding, so it wasn't necessary to bring any.

With the contents of the car transferred to the large hallway beyond the front door, Daddy hugged and kissed each of the children in turn, then hugged and thanked Felicity.

While they all stood on the front steps and watched, he hurried back to the car, reversed it onto the lane and drove past the front of the house, waving from his open window. They all waved back.

'Daddy's really upset,' said Quoia.

'Yes, he is,' said Aunt Felicity. 'He loves you and so does your mother. You must remember how hard this is for them both. Are you all right, Sequoia?'

Kaleb saw that Quoia was crying.

'I will be, Aunt Felicity. It's just sad to see Daddy like that.'

'I understand. Look, let's go inside and get everything sorted. First, though, let's talk about names. You can call me Aunt Felicity when talking about me to Henry or Anna, but for the rest of the time I'd really like it if the three of you would just call me "Fliss." Anything else will just make me feel older than I do already. What do you want me to call you? Sequoia, I've heard Henry refer to you as "Quoia". May I also call you that?'

Quoia smiled and nodded, wiping away her tears.

'Thank you. Jude is the easy one. I've often wished my parents had the sense to give me a name with one syllable rather than four. What about you, Kaleb? Do you shorten your name?'

'No, I like "Kaleb".'

'Very well. Quoia, Jude and Kaleb it is.'

Fliss turned and led the way in through the front door. Once inside, Kaleb looked round at the paintings on the white walls of the broad, welcoming space. What could be seen of the actual floor beneath their belongings was covered in a shiny grey stone. At the far end, five steps climbed up to the full height glass wall at the back of the hall. The stairs then turned back on themselves to ascend to the upper floor. A large panel in the ceiling was made of glass, giving a view up to the level above and letting light pass down into the hall.

'Are the paintings yours, Aunt Felicity, sorry, Fliss?' asked Quoia.

'They are. I do mostly landscapes, though as you can see, I like to bring my own style to them.'

To Kaleb's eyes their aunt's landscapes hanging in the hall seemed very unusual, with lots of bright colours and dark blues. He really liked them.

'I need your help in getting everything put away,' said Fliss. She pointed off to the left as Kaleb was looking, 'On this side of the hall is the main bedroom, which has its own bathroom. That's normally mine, but I thought it best if you have that, Quoia. Along the corridor off to the other side are two further bedrooms, with the main bathroom between them, accessed from the corridor. They are the same size as one another and so are the beds. Jude and Kaleb, you decide between yourselves who's having which.'

'What about you, Fliss?' asked Quoia. 'Where will you sleep?'

'The garage is large enough to have a small apartment above it. I've moved my stuff into there. I know it means I'll be in a different building to you at night, but you'll all be under one roof and I don't see that as a problem. Besides, I'll make sure my number is programmed into your phones. Do you each have a phone?'

The children nodded.

'Alternatively, just come and ring the doorbell if you need me. The door at the far end of the corridor, past the two bedrooms, leads to a small hallway and a back entrance. You can see the door to the apartment and garage from there, across the patio near the back of the side wall.'

'What about keys?' asked Quoia.

'I'll show you where the keys for the back doors are kept later. I've got one spare front door key but haven't been able to get another cut. In the current circumstances I don't see us needing any more. It's not as if we're all likely to be going out separately. Right, I'm assuming the two insulated bags contain food that should go in the freezer?'

Quoia nodded.

'My freezer up in the kitchen is quite full but I've got a large chest freezer out in the garage which has plenty of room. I'll take these bags out.'

'We can help, Aunt Fliss,' said Jude.

'No, that's kind of you, but while I'm doing that you three can be moving your belongings into the bedrooms.'

For some reason, Jude was very keen on having the bedroom nearest the hall. Kaleb didn't mind either way. As far back as Kaleb could remember, Jude had got his way a lot of the time. Mummy and Daddy always tried to be fair when there were arguments, but sometimes that didn't make much difference.

When the boys were younger and Jude had been much bigger that Kaleb, there had been times when he'd got his way by literally pushing his brother around. This had happened less and less lately. That was partly because as Kaleb had grown, Jude had found he no longer had the size advantage that once served him so well. It was also partly because Kaleb was smart enough to find ways of getting Jude to want the result that he, Kaleb, wanted.

Kaleb knew that part of getting what he wanted when it mattered to him was to let Jude think he was getting his way in things that didn't matter. Now was a good example. Jude was obviously extremely pleased to get the bedroom he wanted, leaving Kaleb with the one beyond the bathroom.

Kaleb's bedroom was finished in white, with three of his aunt's paintings around the walls. The bed was wider than the one he had at home. There was a single window, quite wide and not all that deep, and giving a lovely view out over the river, beyond the garden wall and the lane. The built-in wardrobe and the chest of drawers were empty. There was also a small table and a chair. The room was spotlessly clean but had a rather empty feel.

Kaleb was wondering how to organise his things, which were still in bags and boxes on the floor, when there was a knock on the door and Fliss's head appeared round it.

'I'll help you with your unpacking later. For now, I want to move the rest of the food in the hall upstairs to the kitchen and sort out some lunch. Will pizza be OK?'

Kaleb followed Fliss to join Quoia and Jude in the hall and between the four of them they were able to carry the bags and boxes of food upstairs. They left the household stuff where it was. As on his last visit, Kaleb loved the sense of space on the upper floor. The main room, with the kitchen at its rear, rose to a remarkably high ceiling and was partly lit by a series of long windows in the roof.

Much of the light came in through the huge windows at the front of the house, which rose to a point at the tip of the roof. There were also windows on both sides of the far end of the room. The walls were mainly painted white, with available space on them used to display Fliss's paintings. Most of the floor on this upper level was finished in a polished wood effect, like in Kaleb's bedroom downstairs.

'That's amazing,' said Quoia. 'I can see why you called this Forthview House. You are looking right down onto and over the river.'

'Our first idea was to call it The Lighthouse, because it's so light,' said Fliss. 'But friends pointed out that visitors and delivery drivers would never find it because they'd be looking for an actual lighthouse. Forthview House is probably a better name.'

'What's the village you can see over on the other side, on the ridge?'

'That's Clackmannan. You can see the church very clearly, and Clackmannan Tower. It's about two miles away. We look out north-east from here. You can see the line of the Ochil Hills in the distance. Anyway, let's not get distracted by the view. Put the food down over here,' said their aunt. 'I'll check for anything that needs to go in the fridge in a moment but otherwise we can put it away later. Look, I know you've all been here before, but it was a while ago and it might help if I give you a very quick tour of this part of the house.'

Quoia smiled. 'After we were last here, Kaleb was so impressed that he said he wanted to be an architect when he grows up, so he can build somewhere like this and live in it.'

'That's a lovely thought,' said Fliss. 'Who'd have guessed that the world would change so much you'd all end up living here for a while?'

She walked a few paces towards the lounge area that occupied the front half of this end of the upper floor, ending up standing on the glass panel that formed part of the ceiling of the hall below. 'Look, our tour is going to be quite a short one, because you can see most of the upper floor from here.'

It was Jude who asked the question in Kaleb's mind. 'Aunt Fliss, is it safe to stand on that glass? Won't it break?'

Fliss laughed. 'It takes a while to get used to, but it's perfectly safe to walk on, if a little slippery sometimes. When we first moved in, your late Uncle Jim, who was a lot heavier than I am, used to do this when I walked round rather than across the panel.' She jumped in the air and landed with a thud in the centre of the glass. 'Is that proof enough for you, Jude?'

'Yes, Aunt Fliss.'

'Just "Fliss", please. Anyway, as you'll all have seen, the rear end of this part of the house is the kitchen, with a small dining table here. It's big enough for the four of us, which is all we'll need. There are no prizes for guessing that the front half of this end of the upper floor is the main lounge. There's a toilet behind the kitchen, accessed round the side there.

'It's not obvious from the outside, but viewed from above, the main house has a slightly "T" shape, especially on this level. The head of the "T" is occupied by the kitchen and lounge on this floor and by the main bedroom downstairs.'

'The bedroom must be very big, Fliss,' said Kaleb.

'Well spotted Kaleb. Perhaps you do have the makings of an architect. You might have noticed another door towards the rear of the hall, near the bottom of the stairs. That leads to a utility room with the washing machine and tumble drier and central heating boiler in it, and another door to the garden. That's behind my en suite bathroom. It's also where I'm going to put the household stuff you brought with you.'

'Can we see the back garden?' asked Jude.

'Of course. I'll take you out there after lunch. Before we eat, let's finish our brief tour. The double-sided glass fireplace set in this length of wall partly separates the head of the "T" from its tail. As you can see you can walk either side of it. When Jim and I moved in, this end of the space beyond the fireplace was a second lounge area, where he would sit and read or listen to music while I painted in my studio, which made up the rest of that space. With big north-east facing windows it's perfect for me. I usually leave the blinds pulled

20

down over the two back windows to prevent too much sun getting in.

'Over time, my studio has slowly expanded to take over the whole area beyond the fireplace. When I knew you were coming, I had a long overdue tidy up. My studio now takes up maybe two-thirds of that area and I've restored the extra lounge at the near end. As you can see, the far end wall is home to my bookshelves and a desk and computer. Please feel free to borrow and read anything that takes your fancy. You'll find art books, mysteries and historical novels take up a lot of the shelving, though there are many other books there, including some about the area as well as Jim's architecture books, which I kept. I've also dug out and set up Jim's old digital piano at the far end. Your father tells me you're having lessons, Kaleb?'

'Yes, Aunt. Fliss, I mean.'

'As you'll have seen, there's a balcony running along the front of the leg of the "T", overlooking the river and accessed from a door in the side of the front of the lounge. Even though it looks nice out there today, I noticed a chill in the wind while we were outside with your father and the balcony faces north-east. I think that means we may need to wait for another day before enjoying it fully. Something to remember is that the balcony is also our fire escape as there are steps to the ground at the far end, down the side of the house. I've got several fire alarms fitted and a carbon monoxide alarm. If there is an alarm, don't ask questions, simply get out of the house and go over to the riverbank, on the far side of the lane, where you'll not get run over by a fire engine. Only when you are safe should you ring the fire brigade, though the alarms are monitored automatically so they should already be on their way by then.

'I'm sure you'll all be happy to know that we have a good Internet connection here. I've written the Wi-Fi password on a yellow Post-it note that I'll leave on the table, so you can get yourselves connected. There are plenty of sockets for you to charge things. As you'll probably be spending a fair bit of time indoors, it may help you to know that I've got Sky boxes connected to the large television on the lounge wall and to the television downstairs in the main bedroom. Does anyone have any questions?'

Kaleb expected Jude to say something, but there was silence.

Fliss continued. 'Good. I hope that's covered everything and I think I should now sort out lunch. Does anyone want to help?'

Jude and Quoia both helped, while Kaleb started connecting their phones and other devices to Fliss's Wi-Fi.

CHAPTER FOUR

They spent the afternoon settling in. Jude didn't want to unpack his clothes. Kaleb realised that his brother thought that would be like accepting that they would be here for a long time. If he kept his clothes packed and just took out what he needed, then he'd be ready to leave as soon as Daddy came back in the car. It seemed to be Jude's way of trying to keep alive the hope that normality would return sooner rather than later.

Quoia and Fliss gently talked Jude round, pointing out that it would be much easier for him if he put things away properly. What won him over was Fliss saying that he'd still be able to get everything packed again in the time it took Daddy to get here from Kirkliston. When the time came to go home, they'd not be delayed because Jude had unpacked.

Kaleb felt very differently. He had a bigger bed than he was used to in a bigger and better bedroom. He also enjoyed the river view from his window. It was far, far, nicer to look at than the view from his bedroom in Kirkliston. That looked out on their not very large back garden and over other people's gardens to houses that were nice enough but not very interesting. Aunt Felicity's house was every bit as amazing as he'd remembered. He was really looking forward to living here.

He missed his friends, of course. He also missed the

challenge and enjoyment he got from going to his primary school in Kirkliston. But neither of those things were made any different by moving from Kirkliston to Dunmore. Since the lockdown began, he'd not been able to meet his friends, not face to face, or go to school.

It was too soon yet, but Kaleb knew that he would also miss Mummy and Daddy a lot. He knew that Daddy was right, though, that he and Mummy had been away from home much more than usual over the past two weeks. It would help them to know that the children were being properly looked after.

He wondered if Quoia and Jude shared his fear that although the three of them were now safe here, Mummy and Daddy were doing jobs that put them at real risk from the virus. That was one of the things that had allowed Daddy to persuade Mummy to let the children come here.

Kaleb thought he might try to talk to Quoia about it, though only if he could find a moment when Jude wasn't within hearing. He was sure she'd be worried anyway. He didn't want to upset Jude by putting the idea in his head if it wasn't already there.

Jude could sometimes be a little slow in seeing things that were obvious to the others. He and Quoia went to the high school in Queensferry, where Kaleb himself would be going after the summer holidays next year. Quoia had always done very well at school, like Kaleb. Jude did well in some ways but not in others. He was extremely good at anything that needed practical skills, like craft, design and technology. He was also good at sports, and at art. But when it came to academic subjects, he sometimes struggled a little. It was the same at home. He could make and paint plastic models of aeroplanes with a skill that Kaleb envied. But sometimes he needed help from Quoia or their parents with homework that sounded easy to Kaleb.

After tea, Quoia spent some time looking at the books on the shelves at the end of the studio. Fliss had set up an easel for Jude and he was using pencil to sketch the view out over the river.

Kaleb sat in the lounge and played a game on his iPad and then went down to his room to practice on the digital piano, which everyone had agreed should be there rather than in the studio. It wasn't the same type as he had at home, but he quickly got the hang of it. With headphones on, he was soon lost in the music and in his own world. His weekly piano lessons were now done via Skype and the next one was late tomorrow afternoon. He wanted to be able to show that he'd been practising.

He jumped a little when someone touched him on the shoulder. It was Quoia. He stopped playing and took his headphones off.

'Sorry to startle you, Kaleb. Fliss has said that as it's such a lovely evening she's going to take us for a walk. She's convinced Jude that we're allowed to do our daily exercise together as we're all living in the same house.'

'Where are we going?'

'I don't know. She says it will be a surprise. She's said we should wear jackets or fleeces as the wind's still cold and that we should put on our walking boots outside on the front steps.'

*

When everyone was ready, Fliss set the burglar alarm and locked the door. Then she led them out onto the lane through a narrow gate at the village end of the wall running along the front of the garden. Dunmore itself seemed almost as deserted as it had when they'd driven through earlier, though not quite. This time there was an elderly man in a flat hat walking a golden retriever near the bowling club. While keeping his distance, he exchanged a friendly greeting with Fliss and then moved on.

'Do you know him, Fliss?' asked Quoia.

'He's a member of the bowling club. I joined a couple of years ago. I don't bowl much, but it's been good socially.'

'It's a shame we can't have a quick go on the roundabout over there,' said Kaleb.

'That would be against the rules,' said Jude.

Fliss smiled. 'You're both right. Some rules make more sense than others. But avoiding touching objects, like the handrails on the roundabout, that lots of other people might have touched, is one of the more sensible rules.'

A few of the houses and cottages running along the sides of the village green had pieces of paper with coloured rainbows stuck in their windows. Over on the far side of the green, Kaleb saw a girl watching them, through a cottage window that had a rainbow in it. He smiled, then, realising that he was probably too far away for her to see his smile, he raised his hand and waved.

'Who are you waving at?' asked Jude.

'The girl in the window over there, the one watching us.'

'I can't see anyone.'

Kaleb looked again and realised that she had gone. 'Neither can I, now, but she was there. She didn't wave back, though.'

As they walked towards the main road, Jude asked, 'Where are we going, Fliss?'

'I'm taking you to see one of the most amazing buildings in Scotland. It's about a mile from the house, so it's an easy walk for three young and fit people like you. We have to cross the main road, then we go along the track opposite.'

'There isn't much traffic, is there?' asked Quoia. 'It was the same when we were coming here this morning. The motorway was nearly empty.'

'No, you're right,' said Fliss. 'We still need to look carefully, though. Things can come through here quite quickly. That's it, and now we go along this track.'

'With everything else so quiet, you can really hear the birds singing,' said Kaleb.

'Yes, there are some consolations from the lockdown. I think the air's a lot cleaner, for a start. I've seen some people on social media talking about coronavirus as "Gaia's revenge".'

'Who is Gaia?' asked Kaleb.

'She was the ancient Greek goddess who was the mother of all life, the goddess of Mother Earth, if you like. More recently, over the past 40 years or so, the name's been used for a theory that all living things on Earth interact to form a hugely complex system that helps maintain conditions for life on the planet. Some people have been saying that the virus is Gaia's way of controlling the biggest danger to her system, human beings.'

'That's not true, though, is it Fliss?' Kaleb could tell from Jude's voice that he was alarmed at the idea.

Fliss had obviously picked up the same thing. 'No, of course not, Jude. Things have changed far more than we could ever have imagined because of the virus, though. Look above you, what do you see?'

'A blue sky with a few wispy clouds,' said Jude.

'That's right. What would you expect to see?'

'You mean something different? I know. Until the lockdown, we used to see lots of white trails left by high flying aeroplanes on days like this. I suppose you would here too, wouldn't you?'

'That's right, Jude. Condensation trails. We normally get lots over here, mainly made by planes flying from southern England or Europe to North America. There were days when the conditions were right, and the trails didn't just fade away, when they could spread out and almost merge into one another. Now it's a real rarity to see any trails at all, though I think there are still some cargo aircraft crossing the Atlantic.'

'It's even more obvious in Kirkliston,' said Quoia. 'We see the trails, but we also see aeroplanes taking off or landing at Edinburgh Airport. They don't pass over, but they aren't far away, towards Newbridge. It used to be every couple of minutes at certain times of the day. When we've been out on our walks over the last week or so, there have been very few of them. It's like a totally different world.'

'That's very true. Right, when we get to this T-junction of tracks up ahead, we turn left. That's it. Now we follow this track for a while, through this avenue of trees. Incidentally, do you recognise the type of tree, Quoia?'

Kaleb looked ahead. The track they were following had on either side a regularly spaced line of very tall, very straight trees with reddish bark. On the left, behind the line of trees on that side, was a farmer's field, while on the right, again outside the line of trees, the land climbed the slope of a wooded hill. Although the trees on the hillside were only just beginning to show signs of coming into leaf, the tall trees either side of the track were fully green.

Quoia smiled. 'I do, Fliss, and I'm surprised I didn't notice straight away. Mummy and Daddy took us to see some in the Botanic Garden in Edinburgh and I've also seen them in other places. They are Redwoods, or Sequoias.'

'That's right, Quoia. Given their size, I think these were planted here a long time ago. I thought you might like to see them. I've never asked your father, is there a link between your name and the name of the tree? I think Sequoia is a really lovely name, but it's very unusual so I wondered.'

'Mummy told me when I was small that she'd always loved the name. It's a traditional Cherokee girl's name which means "sparrow". The tree is named after a man with the male version of the same name, spelled S-e-q-u-o-y-a-h. He lived from the late 1700s to the early 1800s and invented the Cherokee written language. When they named the tree, they must have decided it should have the female version of his name.'

'What a nice story!' said Fliss.

The track they were following curved round to the right and then petered out. Fliss then led them along a path through a wood that was loud with the sound of birdsong. This had clumps of blue and white flowers growing beneath trees and bushes that, like those Kaleb had seen on the wooded hillside, were just showing the first signs of leaves starting to appear.

Another path brought them to a tall brick wall. There was a small car park a short distance off to one side which had closed gates and a sign that from this distance Kaleb guessed told people to go home. There was a stone gateway in the brick wall blocked by an ornate green metal gate topped off by sharp-looking arrowheads. The two halves of the gate were closed and as they walked up to it, Kaleb could see there was a new-looking padlock and chain holding them together and preventing anyone passing through. There was a sign on one side of the gate saying the garden was closed because of coronavirus.

'The gate's locked!' he said.

'Yes, it is, Kaleb. The walled garden is closed and so is the car park. They want to deter people from travelling to visit attractions like this as part of the virus restrictions. But the gate can's stop you seeing what's beyond it. Be careful not to touch it, though, especially the lock and chain. Why don't you all have a look?'

Kaleb looked through the vertical metal rods forming the gate and could see a straight track leading beyond it to another gateway in what seemed to be a matching wall quite some distance away. On the left of the track was a grassy area that sloped gently down towards trees.

But it was the other side that really caught Kaleb's attention. The ground rose gently on the right and it looked like an orchard of small trees had been planted in another grassy area not far from the gate. Even if they had been in leaf, the trees wouldn't have blocked the view too badly. Beyond them Kaleb could see the roof of what he guessed was a long two storey building running along the top side of the garden. He only saw this after spending some time looking at the much more obvious feature, a circular stone tower ringed by decorations and windows that was topped off by a huge stone pineapple.

'That's amazing!' said Jude, echoing Kaleb's thoughts.

'It is,' said Fliss. 'Remember what I said about not getting too close to the gate and not touching it. It's easy to forget when you are looking at something that spectacular. I promised you one of the most amazing buildings in Scotland and I hope you agree that I kept my promise. That's the Dunmore Pineapple.'

'Is there any way of getting closer?' asked Kaleb. 'I'd love to see more of it.'

'Until the lockdown, the garden was open every day and

you could go right up to the Pineapple and even into a sort of pavilion underneath it,' said Fliss. 'I know that there are other ways into the walled garden and I'm sure if we put our minds to it, we could find a way in. But it wouldn't be the right thing to do when they so very obviously don't want us in there. Besides, there's no need. The Pineapple is normally rented out as a holiday let and the access is via a track round the other side of it. We walked on part of it on our way here. I don't think anyone will be staying there at the moment and we should be able to get a closer look from that side without breaking any rules.'

CHAPTER FIVE

It turned out that it was possible to get reasonably close to the far side of the Dunmore Pineapple by going round the outside of the walled garden. Kaleb had been simply mesmerised by the building. Jude had quickly seen enough, though, and was soon asking Fliss if they could set off back.

When they got to the track leading towards the Redwood avenue, Kaleb asked Fliss how old the Pineapple was.

'I can show you some online references and books that talk about it when we get home,' she said. 'Your Uncle Jim was fascinated by the history of the place. It was one of the things that originally drew him to Dunmore. When we found the plot overlooking the river for sale it seemed ideal. We were able to explore the area after we moved here but sadly, he didn't have all that long to enjoy our new house after it was built.'

'Do you mind me asking what happened?' asked Quoia. 'They might have thought we were too young at the time, but Mummy and Daddy never said much about him.'

'I'm afraid he simply died of a heart attack while visiting a client. It was totally unexpected. He was a heavy smoker and they said that might have been the cause.'

'I'm sorry,' said Quoia. 'It must feel strange living in the house he designed on your own.'

'Not really. It's quite reassuring in a way. It makes me feel that I'm still close to him. And in more normal times I have friends visiting and staying quite a lot. I also run an art club from home, though not now, obviously. There's no point living with regrets and Jim would have wanted me to enjoy living in his house. And now the three of you are sharing it with me and I'm sure he'd have loved the idea of that.'

'Daddy said you are a smoker too, or that you used to be,' said Quoia. 'But you've not smoked since we arrived.'

'I was, but I stopped when Jim died. He'd cut down a lot, we both had, when we moved to the house. We agreed that we'd only smoke in a wooden gazebo we put up in the garden, so we kept the house fresh. But it seems it was too late in his case.'

'I don't really remember Uncle Jim very clearly,' said Quoia. 'Would you have any photographs at home that you'd mind me seeing?'

'Me too,' said Jude and Kaleb, almost together.

Fliss laughed. 'I'd love to show you what I've got, though you'll have to promise to tell me if you get bored! I'll dig them out tomorrow. Look, you can check on the history of Dunmore Park when we get home if you want, but I did learn quite a lot from Jim so can tell you a little while we're walking back.'

'Yes please, Fliss,' said Kaleb.

'All right. Well the story starts just over 500 years ago, and it starts just over there.' They had reached the part of the track running through the Redwood avenue and passing the wooded hillside, now off to the left. Fliss was pointing up the slope.

Kaleb looked and could see that at the top of the slope, probably invisible from here when the trees were fully in leaf, was a stone tower, or part of one. He'd not noticed it on the outward walk. It looked like the right-hand side had collapsed.

'Is that a castle?' he asked.

'It is. It's usually called Elphinstone Tower, but I've also heard it called Elphinstone Castle or Dunmore Tower. It's in a pretty sorry state and there isn't much left beyond a vaulted ground floor room that was later used as a place to bury members of the family that owned it, and one side of the tower.'

'Can we go there?' asked Jude.

'We can have a look on our next walk. There's a path through the wood and up the side of the ridge. It can also be reached by following the edge where the trees meet the farmer's field a little way back, and then round. We should be heading home now, though. Let's walk while I talk.'

Kaleb could see that Jude wanted to protest but thought better of it.

'Anyway, the tower was built by the Elphinstone family in 1510. They owned the estate covering this area, including where the village is. The original tower house was extended sometime later. In 1754 the whole estate was purchased by the 4th Earl of Dunmore, John Murray, for £16,000. I think that would be a huge amount in today's money.

'Seven years later, in 1761, John Murray built the Dunmore Pineapple as a birthday present for his wife Charlotte. The family used it as a summerhouse from which they could view the walled garden of what by that time had become known as Dunmore Park. I think they still lived in the extended castle on the ridge back there which, I suppose, they would have called Dunmore Tower.

'Between 1820 and 1825 the next in line, George Murray, the 5th Earl of Dunmore, built an enormous mansion whose ruins lie a few hundred metres to the north-west of the tower. This was known, a little confusingly, as Dunmore Park, like the estate itself. He also built a large stable block a little

34

further away, which is now also ruined.

'In the middle of the 1800s the family replaced an existing village called Elphinstone Pans with the estate village we know as Dunmore. That's why most of the houses in the village seem to look so good together. The old village had been used as a harbour to ship out the coal that was mined on the estate. You can still see where the harbour used to be. The name "pans" also suggests that it was a place where they extracted salt from the water of the River Forth. They did that by putting sea water in large metal pans that they lit coal fires underneath, evaporating away the water and leaving the salt.'

'That must have been a really dirty process,' said Quoia.

'I'm sure it was,' said Fliss. 'Some time after Dunmore Park was built, the Murrays also demolished later additions to the old tower we were looking at and built a church next to it. As I already said, they used what was left of the tower as a family vault for their dead. In more recent times the church has been demolished and the vault broken into. I hope that was after the bodies that were in it were safely moved.'

'But what happened?' asked Kaleb. 'We saw that the tower was a ruin. But you said the mansion they built is also now in ruins, and the stable block. You make it sound like all that's left is the village and the Pineapple.'

'Well there's also a parsonage, not far from the Pineapple. By most standards that's also a pretty grand house and these days it's used for weddings and events. Well, when things get back to normal, anyway. But basically, you're right, Kaleb.'

'How could that happen?'

'The Earls of Dunmore, the Murray family, continued to live at Dunmore Park until 1911. Presumably, they then sold the estate. Dunmore Park stayed in use as a private home until 1961. It was then taken over by a girls' school for a short time before being abandoned in 1964. In 1970 the whole estate was broken up into lots and sold off. One lot, which included the walled garden and the Pineapple, was then donated to the National Trust for Scotland.

'Two years later, in 1972, parts of Dunmore Park, the mansion, were demolished. Since then various schemes to redevelop what remains of the house and the surrounding area have come to nothing. In 1987 permission was given for complete demolition of the house, but that came to nothing either. Meanwhile mother nature, Gaia if you prefer, is steadily reclaiming the ruins, which have trees growing everywhere now.' Fliss stopped walking for a moment and smiled. 'You are going to ask if we can visit the ruins of the house, aren't you Jude?'

'I was, Fliss. Can we?'

'The place is in a fairly dangerous state, especially with hidden drops and holes where floors should be, sometimes concealed by vegetation. I will take you. But I'd like you all to promise that you'll not visit Dunmore Park or Elphinstone Tower on your own, without me. I don't want to have to explain to your parents how one of you has broken a leg or worse.'

She looked around and seemed satisfied when each of them said that they promised. 'Right, that's us back at the main road. We need another good look despite how quiet it is. Fortunately, there's nothing to block your view of any traffic on this slight bend.'

*

After they were back at Forthview House, everyone washed their hands in the sink in the utility room. Fliss then poured soft drinks and prepared a snack of cheese and biscuits.

Quoia texted their mother and the three children set up a Skype call to her. She looked tired and said that Daddy was still on duty at the hospital. Kaleb started to tell Mummy about how wonderful Fliss's house was. But he could tell that her mind wasn't really on what he was saying so he said much less than he'd planned.

Their mother reminded them that the next day they'd have to spend some time on schoolwork. She told Kaleb that she'd had a message cancelling his piano lesson the following afternoon. The next one would be next week. At the end of the call, she told them how much she loved them. Kaleb could see that she was trying not to cry.

They were all very quiet after the call finished.

Fliss asked about their normal bedtimes and suggested they watch a film. The children had bought a selection of DVDs with them but after a little discussion they agreed to watch a film of Fliss's called *Sunshine on Leith.* They ended up singing along to a lot of the Proclaimers songs and joined in with the dance at the end.

It was much later than his normal bedtime when Fliss and Quoia took him to his room and wished him goodnight. Despite that, Kaleb spent some time standing by the window looking out at the lights beyond the River Forth, wondering if there were children in houses over there looking back in his direction. He thought about what had happened today, thinking especially about the Pineapple and about the girl he had seen in the window of the cottage in the village, the one who had disappeared when he tried to point her out to Jude. Kaleb got into bed very tired but happier than he had been since his school had closed.

CHAPTER SIX

THURSDAY THE 2ND OF APRIL 2020

Kaleb slept in next morning. When he went up to the kitchen, he found Quoia and Jude eating cornflakes while Fliss was cutting a piece of toast. She paused to get a bowl of Rice Krispies for Kaleb and then sat down to spread marmalade on her toast.

'The weather forecast for today is pretty good,' said Fliss. 'It should be quite like yesterday with a fair bit of sun and perhaps a chilly wind. It's a Thursday so I think the three of you should spend the morning on your schoolwork. I'd already talked to Henry about this and after your Skype chat with her last night, while we were watching the film, I had a text conversation with your mother. She tells me you know what you are meant to be doing for the next few days.'

'Do we have to, Aunt Fliss?' asked Jude. 'You said you'd take us to see the old castle and the house.'

'Yes, you do have to, Jude. But if I'm happy that you've been working this morning then I promise to take you all out for a walk this afternoon.'

'And you'll take us to the ruined castle and to the house?' asked Jude.

'Yes, I will, Jude. First, though I need to go out for a little while. I've finished a commission for a client who lives in Stirling. I was meant to take it over yesterday, but I put it off because of your arrival.'

'What is it, Fliss?' asked Quoia.

There was a pause, as if Fliss was surprised to be asked. 'It's a painting of Stirling Castle. It's not all that big, but it was done from a favourite photograph of theirs and they are keen to have the finished picture.'

Fliss looked at the children. As if reading Kaleb's mind, she went on. 'Don't worry, I'll make sure I stay socially distanced from them when I make the delivery. And they've already paid me online, so I'll not be taking any cash they've handled. It will be perfectly safe.'

'Can we see the picture, Fliss?' asked Quoia.

Kaleb thought his aunt looked uncomfortable.

'I'm afraid I wrapped it up a couple of days ago, when I was sure it was dry.' As if changing the subject, Fliss went on, 'Look, where I'm going is on the north side of Stirling, not far from a large Sainsbury's. We could do with more milk if you're going to have cereals for breakfast every morning. And more cereals for that matter. You've had a chance to see what we've got in now. Is there anything else you think I should get while I'm there? I'll check to see if they've got toilet rolls in stock, of course.'

Jude and Quoia came up with a few ideas of things they needed. Then Fliss ran through with the children what they were meant to be doing that morning. With that done and having checked they knew where her mobile number was on the contact lists on their phones, Fliss went downstairs.

Kaleb went to Fliss's computer at the far end of the studio and opened up Sumdog, so he could do some maths and spelling practice. Fliss had switched her computer on earlier.

Quoia sat at the dining table and opened her laptop. 'Come on, Jude. Your laptop's here. Let's get you set up with one of the lesson plans from the home study hub on the school website.'

'I'll be there in a minute. I want to wave goodbye to Fliss, first. You can't see her car on the drive from the lounge because of the balcony. I'll go out to the far end so she can see me wave.'

'OK, but don't be long. We need to show Fliss that we can be trusted to get on with our work. Kaleb's already working down at the other end.'

'He would be, wouldn't he! It's all right for him, and for you. You both find it easy,' said Jude.

There was the sound of a door closing and Kaleb looked up to see Jude walking along the broad balcony that passed in front of the second sitting area and studio. Then he turned back to the computer. Kaleb knew that Jude sometimes got frustrated over his problems with his schoolwork.

A few minutes later Jude was back in the lounge. Kaleb heard him talking to Quoia.

'I don't think that Aunt Fliss was telling the truth about why she was going out.'

'Why not?' asked Quoia.

'I got to the end of the balcony just as she came out through the gate between the house and the garage. I said hello and waved but she didn't seem pleased to see me there. She looked up and seemed a little shocked. It took a moment for her to smile and wave back.'

'Perhaps she was thinking about something else,' said Quoia. 'Perhaps she's so used to living here on her own that it was a shock to see someone on the balcony?'

Kaleb had walked through to join his brother and sister.

'It wasn't just that,' said Jude. 'She was carrying her handbag and a plastic carrier bag partly rolled up, as if there wasn't too much in it. She didn't have a painting with her.'

'Maybe she put it in her car earlier, before making us breakfast,' said Quoia.

'I suppose,' said Jude.

Kaleb could tell that Jude wasn't very convinced. He returned to Fliss's computer at the far end of the studio and put the painting out of his mind.

*

Fliss was back by late morning. She had some shopping with her and Quoia helped her carry it up from the car. Fliss got Jude to hold the front door open for them. In the kitchen she wiped down her purchases, then instructed Quoia to wash her hands before she did so herself.

'I'm sorry it took me longer than expected. There was a queue outside Sainsbury's. People were meant to stand two metres apart, but ideas of what amounted to two metres varied a lot. I got what we needed, though, even a large pack of toilet rolls. I used hand sanitiser before getting into the car, so that should be all right.'

'Why are toilet rolls so hard to find, Fliss?' asked Jude. 'I saw on some news Mummy was watching that there's no problem with the supply of them. And everyone knows that the virus doesn't mean you need more toilet paper.'

'That's a good question. I think it's a sort of mass panic. Someone, somewhere, probably in a newspaper that cares more about its sales or its website clicks than the truth, talked about a shortage. That was enough to cause a shortage when there wasn't one to start with, because everyone suddenly began to buy more than they needed. And before you say it, Jude, I know I've just done the same. The thing is that when something like that happens, you have to join in, or you miss out. That way we all become part of the problem.'

Kaleb wondered if Jude was going to ask about the painting Fliss said she had been taking to a client, but he didn't.

Having discussed their progress that morning, Fliss suggested they could spend the time until lunch doing some art.

'I might have mentioned that in more normal times I run an art club from home. There are some folding easels under the desk that Kaleb's been working at. They've got telescopic legs so they don't take up much space. There are two folding chairs over there, too, as well as mine and the one by the desk.'

'What should we do?' asked Quoia.

'I want to carry on with my drawing of the view over the river,' said Jude.

'That's great, Jude. I could give you something to use for inspiration, Quoia. There are books showing the work of any number of artists on the shelves. You could use one as the basis for a drawing. We've probably not got time for paint this morning.'

'Do you have anything about the French Impressionists?'

'Yes, though with them the paint is probably the most important thing. Having said that, I'm sure you could find something to use. What about you, Kaleb?'

'I've brought a book with me that shows spaceships and other vehicles from the Star Wars films. Could I use one of them to try to draw from?'

'Of course. It's not the subject that's important for learning, it's what you do with it. If it's something that interests you, then all the better. I've got lots of pencils you can all use, or charcoal, or pastels or crayons if you prefer.'

Kaleb enjoyed drawing a droid control ship based on a picture on a fold-out page in his book. Fliss offered ideas on

42

how he might do the drawing and praised what he produced. She also offered Quoia advice. She spent more of her time with Jude, pointing out things in the view and discussing how his drawing was developing. Kaleb felt a little left out, then wondered if this was Fliss's way of helping Jude get over the disappointment he'd obviously felt after their online lessons.

CHAPTER SEVEN

After lunch they headed out for their walk. Fliss had put some biscuits and a bottle of water in a small pack, with three torches. Jude volunteered to carry it.

There was no sign of the man and his dog today. There was no sign of anyone, in fact. Kaleb looked across at the cottage where he'd seen the girl the previous day, but there was no-one to be seen there either.

There were no pavements beside the lane from the village green to the main road, just a narrow verge and a hedge on one side and the edges of people's gardens on the other. As they reached its start, Kaleb saw a boy and a girl holding a dog on a lead walking towards them. It was the girl he'd seen the previous day. She had long blonde hair and seemed to be about Quoia's age. She wore jeans and a red jumper. The boy looked about the same age as Jude. He had very short blond hair and wore jeans and a black jacket. The dog was a brown cocker spaniel that didn't seem from its size to be all that old.

'Let's cross the road to let them pass safely,' said Fliss.

They went and stood on an area of grass beside a hedge and waited.

'Hello,' said Quoia as the children approached on the opposite side of road.

'Hello,' said the girl, smiling. The boy, who looked as if he might be her brother, smiled as they passed but didn't say anything.

Kaleb wanted to go over to pet the dog but knew that would be against social distancing rules.

Once the children were past, Fliss led the way towards the main road.

'So, there are other children in the village.' said Jude.

'I think those two live over on the far side of the green with their mother and another sister. Their mother isn't a member of the bowling club, so I've never met her to talk to, just seen her occasionally as I've driven past. The gossip in the bowling club is that she got divorced from their father when the children were small and came to live here in their grandmother's house. The grandmother died last year.'

'I saw the girl looking out of a window in one of the cottages over there yesterday,' said Kaleb.

'Other than them,' continued Fliss, 'I've not noticed many children here. You sometimes see two younger ones playing on the swings or the roundabout, usually with their mother sitting on one of the nearby benches with a push chair. But I think that's about it. The arrival in the village of you three will probably be of some interest. Not that it means there's anyone you can play with in these very strange times, of course.'

After crossing the main road, they followed the route they'd taken the previous day, turning left at the T-junction of tracks and walking between the rows of Redwoods. Where the wood on the right ended, Fliss led the way up the edge between it and the field.

After a short climb that led round the back of the wood, Fliss stopped. 'This can get very overgrown with nettles and brambles in summer,' she said, 'but you can now see what we've come to see, Elphinstone Tower.'

Kaleb looked. From this side, the ruin of the tower was

much more obvious. It stood perhaps 50 metres from the edge of the field and there was a trodden-down path leading to it. It was surrounded by a dense growth of conifers, which obscured its base from view.

'It's as if someone's taken a huge axe and sliced down the centre of the tower,' said Jude. 'Everything on the left of the cut has gone, but everything on the right of it is still standing, all the way up to the height of the battlements.'

'It looks like it could blow over next time there's a storm,' said Quoia.

'Who's to say you aren't right?' said Fliss. 'It does look quite precarious from here. I've absolutely no idea how it came to look like that. You'd expect either more of it to be standing or more of it to have collapsed, if you know what I mean.'

Kaleb knew exactly what his aunt meant.

'Can we go and see?' asked Jude.

'Yes, you can, but don't touch anything and don't climb on anything. I'll not be far behind. I'll take the pack from you, but you might find you need one of the torches.'

Jude hurried off towards the tower, carrying a torch. Fliss followed with Quoia and Kaleb. Kaleb understood why Jude was so keen to be the first to get to the tower. But he just wanted to look and to learn and to enjoy visiting somewhere new and different. Rushing around didn't seem the best way to do that.

'There's a broken gravestone there,' said Quoia pointing to the side of the track. 'It's a stone cross lying in the grass next to its base.'

'There's another over there,' said Fliss.

Kaleb walked over to the second stone cross, leaning at an angle against a pile of rubble. 'It's got an inscription,' he said.

'It says, "THY WILL BE DONE" in capital letters. I can't see anything else.'

'That first one's got a longer inscription on the base,' said Quoia. 'It's not complete and parts are obscured by moss, but it commemorates an Anne MacDonald who died in February 1950 and her husband who died a few months later. That's a lot more recent than I was expecting.'

'Me too, if I'm honest,' said Fliss.

'Come and look!' shouted Jude from an arched stone doorway set into the base of the tower. 'This place is seriously creepy!'

Fliss handed Kaleb a torch and he clambered over some mossy stones towards where his brother stood. The interior of the room beyond Jude was very dark. There was a heavy wooden door that stood open and was leaning at an odd angle, like a hinge had been broken. The door had rows of big nails with square, pointed heads driven into it, as if to add strength. Kaleb realised that the wooden door was backed by a heavy metal door, which also stood open.

'Look in here,' said Jude. He shone his torch around the room beyond.

Kaleb switched his torch on and stepped inside.

'The concrete rack on this wall is really deep,' said Jude. 'The compartments go a long way back.'

'Remember what I said about not touching anything,' said Fliss, who had followed them into the room, with Quoia just behind. 'I think those compartments are large enough to take coffins slid in end-on. This is where the family's dead would have been buried.'

'I'm not sure I like the idea of just hiding your dead away in here,' said Quoia. 'It seems, well, like Jude said, creepy. It seems much better to bury people, or to cremate them and to spread their ashes somewhere that meant something to them, like a favourite beach or mountain top. This seems so temporary. Even with a strong door, there's always the chance that people left here will be disturbed later. Everyone buried here must have been disturbed because they're not here now.'

'That's true,' said Fliss.

Jude had gone back outside. Kaleb heard him shout, 'Can I climb up here?'

'Just wait,' called Fliss. 'We'll be out in a moment.'

When Kaleb emerged back into the sunshine, Jude wasn't in sight. Fliss and Quoia came out a moment later.

'Where are you, Jude?' called Fliss.

'Just up here.'

Kaleb looked round and saw that Jude had scrambled up a steep slope that seemed to lead round onto the top of the room they had just been in, within what was left of Elphinstone Tower.

Kaleb looked at Fliss.

'Up you go, Kaleb,' she said, 'if you want to. But be careful. Don't stand under anything that might fall on you.'

Kaleb climbed up to join Jude in what was left of the tower. The insides of the almost complete end wall and the two partial side walls were heavily overgrown and if anything looked more in danger of collapse from here than they had when seen from the outside.

'Come on down now, boys,' said Fliss. Other than some hard to understand features on the ground, we've seen what there is to see here.'

Kaleb climbed back down to where Fliss and Quoia were standing. Jude followed a couple of minutes later.

'Right, Quoia and Kaleb, can you follow the path that runs round the outside of the end wall and down the slope? You'll find it comes out on the avenue of Redwoods. Jude, you just wait a moment.'

As Kaleb followed Quoia he looked back to see Fliss talking quietly to Jude, who didn't seem very happy.

Fliss and Jude caught them up on the track. Jude still looked unhappy.

'Which way now, Fliss?' asked Quoia.

'We should walk back the way we came. When we get to the track that turns right towards the main road, we keep straight on going along the track we've not used before. In case you're wondering, I have just explained to Jude why it's important that you all do as I ask in places like this. I've told him that if he disobeys me again, as he did when he climbed up into the tower, he will be left at home the next time we go out for a walk.'

'I'm sorry, Fliss,' said Jude. 'I just find places like that so exciting.'

'I know, Jude. But as I said, they are also extremely dangerous. It's particularly important that you listen to what I say, and do as I say, when we get to the ruins of the house.'

They followed the track beyond the T-junction until it curved round a corner to the left.

'There's a stone wall on the left along here,' said Fliss. 'We are looking to turn off along a faint path through the trees. It can get really overgrown later in the year, but at the moment it should be easier to find our way and to see what's around us.'

Once they'd left the main track, Fliss led them through trees that seemed very densely packed. Kaleb wondered how it would be possible to find your way with even thicker growth and the leaves out in summer. It didn't take long until the trees ahead of them thinned out and they found themselves among stone shapes on the ground. Kaleb wondered if they were the bases of buildings that had been knocked down.

Then Fliss stopped. Kaleb was immediately behind her and had been looking at where he was putting his feet, so nearly bumped into her.

'Welcome to Dunmore Park,' she said, gesturing ahead.

Kaleb looked past Fliss. He could see a bulky stone ruin rising out of the wood, topped off by groups of decorated chimneys and some narrow turrets. There were no roofs and it was obvious that parts of the house were no longer standing.

'Can I go and look?' asked Jude, who hadn't been far behind.

'It's important we all stay close together while we're here,' said Fliss. 'If we can't do that then we will go straight home and not return. Are we all clear about that?'

The children all nodded.

'Are you sure you'll remember what I've said, Jude?'

'Yes, Fliss.'

'Good. Follow me and we'll get a little closer.'

Fliss stopped again when they reached a point where they were looking down into an open area in the heart of the building, which from here seemed huge.

'Right, the main house had four ranges, built in a square, and these surround an open courtyard, which is what we can see down there. The most substantial part still standing is the range over on the far side, the one whose back we're looking at. That's usually called the south range, though it actually faces rather more south-east.

'That had the main reception rooms of the house, including a drawing room, a dining room, the library and so on. It's where visitors would have been entertained and functions held. Over on our left is the east range, which also still has most of its walls standing. I've seen it said that was where

50

they had the family rooms, including the bedrooms.

'On the right is the west range, which is said to have housed offices, with the main entrance at its far end. There's a fair bit left standing of the part furthest from us, but this end is largely demolished.

'Immediately in front of us is what's left of north range. As you can see, the end of it on our left, where it meets the east range, still has standing walls. Much of it, in front of us and to our right, was demolished in 1972, along with this end of the west range. The north range apparently housed the service functions of Dunmore Park, including the kitchen on the lowest floor and more offices and servants' quarters higher up. Most of the house had two storeys above a basement level but I've seen a picture which suggests there was also an attic level in this range.'

'You can see three levels on the back of the range on the far side,' said Jude.

'That's true, I'd not noticed that before,' said Fliss. 'There was an extra floor, a sort of tower, in the centre of that range, but the extra row of windows you've spotted seems to run the length of it. Perhaps they had lower ceilings and an extra floor on this side.

'It's difficult to get any sense of the northernmost corner of the house now. It looks as if they started demolition at that corner and had proceeded part way along two ranges from there when they stopped. They seem to have simply left the heaps of rubble nearby. You can still see them along here.'

'Where do we go now, Fliss?' asked Jude.

'You've been very patient, Jude. I'll let you decide. We have two choices and we will do both. It's just a question of where we go first. One option is to go round the west side of the house to the entrance. Then we go into the ground floor of the south range and parts of the two side ranges. The other option is to descend the ramp that's just beyond where Quoia's standing into the courtyard, which is at basement level. From there we can explore the basements or cellars of the three ranges.'

'Let's do the cellars first,' said Jude.

'No problem. You lead but remember not to get any distance ahead of us and if I say something, make sure you take notice.'

'Yes, Fliss.'

CHAPTER EIGHT

Jude led them down the ramp and over to the west side of the courtyard, then into a roofless corridor that had dark rooms off to one side, and lighter roofless rooms off to the other. They went into some of the rooms. It all felt incredibly sad to Kaleb.

At the far end of the west range corridor, Jude stopped and turned completely round, looking upwards.

Kaleb, only a short distance behind, walked up to him. 'Wow!' he said as he emerged into another roofless corridor, this one running the length of the basement of the south wing. 'This place is huge.'

The corridor was wide and stone walls rose high on both sides of it, all the way to the top of the building. The two sides were linked at intervals by stone bridges. Every flat surface had vegetation growing from it. There were doors along both sides of the bottom level of the corridor.

'This is where the torches will come in handy,' said Fliss. A lot of these rooms were wine cellars. She led the way through a doorway into a dark space beyond. All the way around the walls were brick structures supporting flat stone surfaces.

'These look like the racks for the coffins in Elphinstone Tower,' said Quoia.

'That's true,' said Fliss, 'but the compartments aren't nearly as deep. Just deep enough to pile bottles of wine on their sides with a little space in front of them.'

'They must have had a lot of wine,' said Kaleb.

'Jim and I once tried to work it out,' said Fliss. 'Each compartment is numbered, and it takes no great genius to realise that if all the compartments in all the rooms down here were full, there could be many thousands of bottles of wine in storage.'

She went back out into the corridor. 'Look, that room leading off the end of the corridor is particularly interesting.' She led the way again. 'This one has eight sides, so it forms an octagon, and there are compartments lining all of the outside walls. You can go round the back of this central support and emerge round the other side. Yes, just like that Jude.'

Fliss shone her torch through a doorway within the central support of the room. 'What I find most fascinating is that there are a few more racks in here. You could imagine this inner room within a room, which you can see once had its own door, was used for storing the best and most expensive wines, where guests and servants couldn't get their hands on them.'

They went back out into the corridor. To Kaleb it felt more like being in a sheer-sided mountain canyon. At the far end they turned left and started to move through the rooms in the basement level of the east wing. They did this until they had reached its north end.

'This part of the house doesn't feel good,' said Quoia. 'I shivered then and part of me just wants to get back up to the edge of the wood.'

'That's silly,' said Jude. 'Look, there's the start of a set of stone steps here. They only go up a short way until they turn back on themselves. Everything above that except for the outer walls has gone.'

'We're in the surviving corner of the north and east ranges here,' said Fliss.

'Can we go, now?' asked Quoia.

Kaleb didn't want to be mocked by Jude, so he said nothing. He understood why Quoia wanted to leave this part of the house. Something felt wrong here. The closer he got to the steps Jude had found, the worse it felt. The sun was shining but he suddenly felt unhappy and afraid.

'Let's move on,' said Fliss. 'The ramp we used to come down into the courtyard isn't far in this direction. Come on Jude, I don't want you climbing those steps. They may look solid enough but that's no guarantee they wouldn't just collapse if someone puts their weight on them.'

Kaleb watched as Jude appeared to bite back a protest. Meanwhile Quoia, needing no second invitation to go, had disappeared out of view. He followed, leaving Fliss with Jude.

Kaleb found Quoia waiting at the top of the ramp. She had her arms wrapped around herself.

'Are you all right, Quoia?'

Quoia smiled. 'I am now, but I really didn't like it down there by the bottom of those steps.'

'I know what you mean,' said Kaleb.

'Did you feel something too?'

'I just had a really strong feeling that something wasn't right when I got near them. I didn't say anything because of Jude. He'd have made fun of me. I was glad when you moved away because it meant I could follow. I feel fine here.'

'I do too,' said Quoia, 'now I've stopped shaking.'

'Ah, here you are,' said Fliss. 'Right, the next part of the tour is to go round the far side and into the ground floor through the main entrance. Is everyone happy with that?'

'That sounds brilliant,' said Jude.

Quoia smiled. 'You lead on, Fliss. We'll follow.'

There was a well-trodden path round the outside of the

ruin, in places passing piles of demolition rubble.

'Watch where you're putting your feet,' said Fliss. 'There are quite a few places along the outside of the walls of the house where the ground simply drops away, I suppose originally that was to provide light to windows at cellar level. Follow the path and keep clear of the walls to stay safe. Right, this is the main entrance we're coming up to.'

'It's amazing,' said Kaleb. 'It sticks out from the side of the house.'

'I can't remember the technical name, but it was intended to allow horses and carriages to drive in and stop under cover and let people get into the house without getting wet if it was raining,' said Fliss. 'Here, inside the front doorway, is the entrance hall. It's octagonal, which I think means it must be above the same-shaped room that we saw in the cellars.

'Let's look first at the west range. There's not a huge amount to see, and you must be careful because the floor just stops after a short distance and there's a sheer drop to the level below.'

Fliss led them through, then back to the entrance hall. 'The front rooms of the south range are rather more complete at this ground floor level. Let's go through that way.'

The building was just a shell, two storeys high except for its centre section, which was three. It was open to the sky. Kaleb loved the scale of the rooms and the detail he could still see. 'There's an old metal fireplace up there, which must have been in an upstairs room. And you can still see wall plaster in places. Look at that column over there.'

'I find the huge stone window frames the most amazing thing,' said Quoia. 'You can easily imagine them with glass in.'

'You can,' said Fliss. 'Less good is that these metal beams

running between the front and back walls seem to be holding the house up. What I find most sad is the way that nature is reclaiming the place. It's less obvious now, when the leaves aren't out, but there are trees growing just about everywhere. Their roots must be doing a lot of damage to the structure. Part of me would love to see this place restored as a hotel or something. Another part of me wonders whether the house is now beyond saving. It can only be a matter of time before nature, or Gaia, swallows it up altogether.'

'Where to now?' asked Jude.

'We'll save exploring the ruined stable block for another day,' said Fliss. 'For now, we'll finish off here with a quick look at the ground floor of the east range. Then we'll come back and climb out through that bay window at the end of the south range. There's a path there that leads round the front of the house, then back the way we came.'

Once outside the front of the grandest part of the house, Fliss pointed out the beautifully detailed stone carvings still visible in places. 'Look at that. There's a row of carved coats of arms on shields above the window.'

'They look like they could have been carved yesterday,' said Quoia.

'They are very sharp, like the intricate detail above the higher level of windows. It's just a shame about all this.' Fliss gestured at the small trees growing close to the front wall and out beyond the path they were following.

After they'd returned to the rear of the house, Fliss had no difficulty leading them through the wood. They emerged onto the track that led back towards the main road and village at the point where they'd left it.

It was Quoia who asked the question that had been troubling Kaleb. 'Fliss, have you read anything about

Dunmore Park being haunted?'

'There's no such thing as ghosts,' said Jude. 'Daddy told me once when he was reading to me at bedtime.'

'I'm sure Henry's right,' said Fliss. 'But there are still lots of things people find hard to explain. I'm sure I've read nothing about Dunmore Park being haunted, though. I would have remembered if I had. Why do you ask?'

'I just wondered,' said Quoia. 'It looks the sort of place that might be. I suppose I wondered why they'd pulled down just one corner but left the rest of it still standing. Most of the walls, anyway.'

Fliss laughed. 'You think the demolition workers might have been scared away by ghosts? I'm sorry, Quoia, I don't know. You can see if you can find out when we get back to Forthview House if you like.'

*

After they got back from Dunmore Park, Quoia spent some time looking through Fliss's architecture books and on the Internet for information about the old house. From her occasional comments there was quite a lot available online.

At one point she called everyone to look on her laptop at a film that someone had taken of the house from a drone. It seemed to be taken in winter and was dated a few years earlier. As a result, the trees seemed smaller and thinner and you could see much more of the house than Kaleb expected. Then they went to look at the same film on Fliss's computer at the far end of the studio because it had a larger screen.

Quoia also displayed on Fliss's computer a photograph she'd found that was taken looking down from directly above the house, perhaps from another drone. This seemed to be more recent than the film. Fliss said it might have been taken the previous summer. It certainly showed just how badly overgrown the house had become by trees which were green and leafy in the picture.

A little later, with Fliss and Jude out of earshot, Quoia told Kaleb that she'd not found anything about the house being haunted.

In the evening they had a Skype conversation with Mummy and Daddy. Kaleb thought how tired they both looked. They tried to be cheerful, but it didn't seem very natural. Nobody said anything about it, but Kaleb got the sense that Quoia was quite worried by the way their parents appeared.

Later, Fliss suggested they could watch another of her films, *The Greatest Showman*. Again, there had been music to sing along to, which Kaleb enjoyed. In the middle of the film, Fliss said there was something she needed to do and went downstairs. After she'd been gone for a while, Quoia stopped the film and said they'd better check that Fliss was all right.

They couldn't find her downstairs or in the garden, so Quoia and Kaleb went to the door to the apartment Fliss was using and pressed the doorbell. It took Fliss a while to open the door and when she did, she looked angry. When she saw them, she smiled and said she was sorry she'd worried them. Behind her, Kaleb could see stairs leading upwards, he guessed to the apartment. There was also a door to the side that he thought must be a back way into the garage.

Fliss said she would be back upstairs very shortly and suggested they carry on watching the film. Quoia and Kaleb returned to the lounge where Jude was playing a game on his laptop.

They told Jude that they'd found Fliss.

'I think she's got someone else staying in the apartment,'

said Jude.

'Don't be silly!' said Quoia. 'What on earth makes you think that?'

'I don't believe she was doing what she said yesterday. None of us saw her come back from Stirling.'

'I helped her bring the shopping up from the car,' said Quoia.

'Yes, but you can't see the drive from the lounge. It would have been easy enough for someone to get out and go up to the apartment before she got you to help with the shopping. Did either of you actually see her arrive back so we can be sure there was no-one else in the car?'

'I really do think you are being silly, Jude. But if that's what you think then you should ask Fliss about it.'

Fliss joined them a little later. Kaleb got the feeling that she felt awkward that they'd been so worried about her that they'd come to find her.

After the film, Fliss read to Kaleb in his room. The others now thought they were too old to be read to.

CHAPTER NINE

FRIDAY THE 3ᴿᴰ OF APRIL 2020

It took Kaleb a little while to remember where he was when he woke up. When he did, he smiled. He got out of bed and raised the roller blind that had been covering his bedroom window.

There was a bit more cloud this morning than there had been since they'd arrived, but it was still a nice day. Kaleb looked out over the river. He didn't think he would ever get bored of this view. It was even better from upstairs, he reminded himself. He should get dressed and go and find the others.

Kaleb was again the last to get to the kitchen for breakfast.

Afterwards, Fliss set them off on schoolwork, with Jude and Quoia on their laptops at the dining table and Kaleb on the computer at the far end of the studio. She then settled down to carry on with a painting that Kaleb had noticed on her easel the previous day.

'Where's that, Fliss?' he asked.

'It's a place called Sandwood Bay. It's in the far north-west of Scotland.'

'Have you ever been?'

'A long time ago. The beach is four miles from the nearest road, so it's quite a walk. I went with Jim and with Belinda and Michael when they were much younger. We were staying in a rented house in a fishing village not far away. It was a lovely day when we set off, but bad weather came in on the way back. We were absolutely soaking when we got back to where we'd parked. It was still a magical day, though.'

'Is that why you are painting it?'

Fliss smiled. 'No, this isn't for me. It's a commission. It's being done as a present for a couple who love the place too. Their daughter has let me have a photograph they took of the bay and I'm basing the painting on that.'

'What's that, at the far end?'

'Ah, that's one of its most remarkable features. It's a sea stack that stands by cliffs at the southern end of the bay. As a result, you couldn't mistake the view as being of anywhere else. Look, this is the photograph, on my iPad. As you can see, I've put a grid over it to help with composition. What do you think of what I've done so far?'

'It makes it seem more dramatic,' said Kaleb. 'I like your paintings because they seem to give the places in them a lot of life. I know you've got a way to go, but this looks really good.'

'Thank you, Kaleb,' said Fliss. 'I hope they like it, too. My paintings sometimes aren't to everyone's taste.'

'I'm sure they will,' said Kaleb.

Fliss stopped painting a few times to go and talk to Quoia and Jude about what they were doing, and to check Kaleb was happy with his progress. After they'd been working for two hours, she set Quoia and Jude to continue with the art projects they'd been working on the previous day.

'Can I draw something else out of my Star Wars book?' asked Kaleb.

'You can if you want. Otherwise, I can let you look at the plans and drawings that Jim did of Forthview House and photographs taken after it was built. If you are going to be an architect when you are older, you'll need to be able to draw buildings. I'd like to give you a commission, which is to do a drawing of the house as it would appear to someone on a boat on the river. How does that sound?'

'It sounds great,' said Kaleb.

Fliss again spent time talking to each of them about what they were doing and how they might best get the results they wanted. The three children carried on while Fliss made toasted ham and cheese sandwiches for lunch.

By the time lunch was ready, Kaleb thought he had made a good start on the drawing Fliss had asked him to do. She certainly seemed happy with what he had done.

After lunch, Jude and Kaleb did the washing up, though there wasn't very much of it.

'Why don't you have a dishwasher, Fliss?' asked Jude.

'I think they're more trouble than they are worth, to be honest,' said Fliss. 'By the time you've loaded and unloaded one, you might as well have done the washing up yourself. Besides, we had one in our house in Stirling before we moved here, and it was always very noisy and seemed to take forever. I didn't want to have to sit in the lounge and listen to the dishwasher doing its thing.'

'OK,' said Jude. 'It's not a problem at home because the kitchen is separate. But I do know what you mean. Fliss, now we've done the washing up, can we go out for a walk again?'

'I don't think it's particularly warm, but yes, a walk would probably do us all good.'

'You said we could explore the stable block near the big house on our next walk.'

'I did say something like that, Jude. But I think we might go somewhere a little different today. It will mean driving five miles on back roads, but I thought that today I'd take you to see a real castle and a couple of other things I'm sure you'll find interesting.'

'We're not really meant to drive anywhere unless it's really necessary, are we?' asked Jude.

'No, we're not, Jude,' said Fliss. 'But it's not far and it is to allow us to take our permitted daily exercise. That makes it acceptable.'

Kaleb had the feeling that Fliss had said that to make Jude feel better about the walk rather than because it was true. But he liked the idea of visiting a castle, so didn't say anything. He noticed that Quoia also made no comment. Perhaps, he thought, she liked the idea of going somewhere other than Dunmore Park.

*

Fliss pulled her car off the road onto a slightly muddy area immediately in front of a ruined single storey stone building. There was another car parked a little ahead of them. On the opposite side of the road was a white bungalow.

'How far are we walking, Fliss?' asked Jude.

'If we do everything I have in mind, it's under three miles. Perhaps a mile of that is a bit of a detour that we can leave off if we want to. Like yesterday I've put some biscuits and water in a pack, with a couple of torches, though I don't think we'll need them. We will need our coats though, because it's not especially warm, even though it looks nice. And you've already got your boots on. I think that's everything.'

They gathered at the back of the car and Fliss locked it. She then led them a few metres back to a track that headed slightly uphill, away from the road they'd parked beside.

After walking a short distance up the track, she turned right onto a path that had a wooden signpost at its start, pointing to 'Tappoch Broch'.

She stopped. 'Well this is all quite different. Last time I was here, before Jim died, this path went straight into an extremely dense conifer forest. It looks like they've cleared the trees since then. The signpost is also new, which is a help. Last time we needed to use a GPS to follow the path, which was tricky under the cover of the trees. I expected to have to do the same this time.'

Kaleb looked around as they followed the path across a slope, surrounded by the low stumps of felled trees. It didn't take long until they came to the edge of the forest that hadn't been cleared. Just inside the wood they moved off the path to allow an elderly couple walking the other way to pass. Everyone exchanged greetings.

The path through the trees continued its gentle climb. To Kaleb this seemed a lovely place. After a while, the trees cleared ahead of them and he could see a mound, covered in heather and dead bracken.

'What is this, Fliss?' asked Quoia.

'It's Tappoch Broch, as you'll have seen on the sign back there. It's sometimes also called Torwood Broch. Who can tell me what a broch is?'

'I can,' said Kaleb. 'We were on holiday on the Isle of Skye last year. We visited a place on the mainland using a little ferry with a car deck that turned to allow you to drive on and off. There was a dog, a collie, that seemed to spend its day travelling backwards and forwards with the ferry.'

'I remember that,' said Jude. 'Mummy and Daddy took us to two brochs not far from the ferry that you reached along a very narrow road. One was quite tall and cut away. A bit like Elphinstone Tower. It meant you could see what was inside the walls. The other one, further along the road, was a more complete circle, but wasn't as tall. But those were made of stones piled up. Mummy said they originally had a shape like the power station cooling towers we'd seen being demolished on TV. This is just a mound. It doesn't look anything like those brochs.'

'That's true,' said Fliss. 'But follow me up and you might be able to see some similarities.'

Fliss led them to the top of the mound.

'It's like a volcano,' said Kaleb. 'It's a cone with a crater cut into the top.'

'I'd not thought of that,' said Fliss, 'but I can see what you mean. Look, there's a path all the way round the top and, as you say there's a crater that's a few feet lower in the middle. If you look, you can see beneath all the heather and other vegetation that the inner walls are made of stone that's been piled up.'

'Those are more like the walls in the brochs we saw,' said Jude.

'That's right,' said Fliss. 'You have to think of this as the lowest part of a broch that was built on the top of the hill here that might have been ten metres or more in height. The outsides of the walls have been buried over the centuries and everything above what you see has been lost.

'As you've been to the brochs at Glenelg you'll probably know that there are about 500 brochs in Scotland, all built around 2,000 years ago. What makes this one out of the ordinary is that most of them are in the north or west of the country. It's very unusual to find one in central or southern Scotland. What's also interesting is that it's close to the line of a Roman Road that ran from near Falkirk up towards Stirling. You can't see because of the forest, but it passed by only a couple of hundred metres from here and the broch must have been obvious to Romans using the road.'

'Perhaps they sold refreshments to travellers and Roman soldiers on the road,' said Kaleb.

Fliss laughed. 'You know, that might be a good idea Kaleb. We'll probably never know. As I said, not much remains of the broch, but you can see the bottom few steps of the staircase that would have run up through the walls to the top, and you can also see the entrance, over by where you are standing Jude. Does anyone want a biscuit or a drink of water while we explore?'

After they'd spent some time looking at the broch, Fliss led the way along a different path, though again one that ran through areas where the forest had been cleared. They emerged onto a track close to another wooden signpost.

'Right, we now have a choice,' said Fliss. 'It's not far from here to Torwood Castle, which we can visit. You can't go inside but it's interesting to look at anyway. Alternatively, we can keep that until a little later and take a diversion along a path that runs between the wood and the field over there. Just over half a mile down there is the Torwood Blue Pool, a mysterious brick-lined circular blue pool that is hidden away in the forest.'

'I vote for the pool,' said Jude.

'Me too,' said Quoia and Kaleb together.

Fliss led them along a path that ran between a wall beside the forest and a fence separating it from the field. Kaleb wondered how they'd stay distanced from anyone they met on it, but as it happened, they saw no-one.

When they reached the first of two lines of power cables running across the field on their left on huge pylons, Fliss led them into the forest along a gap that had been left for the pylons.

'And this is the blue pool,' said Fliss, pointing ahead.

Kaleb could see a low circle of bricks set into the ground, on the edge of the forest and partly hidden by a tree. The bricks enclosed a pool of water that lived up to its name by being quite blue. There were lots of sticks and leaves and conifer needles floating on the surface and his first reaction was to feel a little disappointed.

'What is it?' asked Quoia.

'That's a good question,' said Fliss. 'The best theory I've seen is that it's a relic of an old coal mine whose main workings were about a mile away to the north-west. You might remember what I said about coal being mined on the estate. Well this whole area formed a large coalfield, though the mines on this side of the River Forth have all long gone. The last deep coal mine in Scotland was only about five miles east of Forthview House, on the north side of the river. It closed in 2002.

'The mine near here closed much earlier, in 1910. This brick circle seems to be the top of a shaft built to allow the mine workings to be ventilated and it flooded when the mine was abandoned. I've seen it said that local children swim in the pool. It's a bit chilly today and looking at the muck floating on top of the pool I'm not sure I fancy the idea anyway. Do any of you want to give it a go?' Fliss looked at Jude and smiled.

'No thanks, Fliss,' he said. 'We can all swim, but I don't like the look of that.'

'I think that's very sensible, Jude. Now, if you've seen enough here, let's go to that castle I promised you.'

Fliss suggested Jude lead as they went back the way they had come up the path between the field and the forest. When they reached the track at the end of the path, she gave the boys directions to get to the castle. Jude and Kaleb ran off, leaving Fliss to follow with Quoia. They'd had good views of Torwood Castle across the fields from the path leading to and from the pool and Kaleb found the idea of getting closer to it exciting.

What they found was a large and impressive building, though it looked a little odd when seen with the blades of a wind turbine rotating beyond it. As they approached, Kaleb saw a young couple standing off to the right. They were looking up at something and after a moment Kaleb realised that they were flying a drone that went over the castle before returning to them. The boys stood some distance away and watched.

'What do you think of the castle?' asked Fliss as she joined them with Quoia.

'It makes me think a little of Dunmore Park,' said Kaleb. 'It's not as ruined, but it's been taken over by trees in the same way. It doesn't seem very cared for.'

'I did read that someone was trying to do it up,' said Fliss, 'but it would be a huge job.'

'Can we go inside?' asked Jude.

'As I said earlier, I think probably not. If I remember rightly, the only entrance is in the angle of the main tower over here. Yes, look. It's firmly closed with a metal door that someone's spray-painted graffiti on. We can walk round the outside, though. It's quite an interesting building because it's so complete. I know there are no roofs in place, but it's surprising that the walls all seem to be standing up to their full height.'

After they'd done a clockwise tour of the outside of the castle, they gave the couple still flying the drone plenty of space as they passed them by.

'Is that it?' asked Jude. 'Have we visited everywhere?'

'Yes, we have,' said Fliss. 'It's just a gentle downhill stroll along this track back to where we parked the car.

'It's been a nice walk, Fliss, thank you.'

You're welcome, Jude. Tell me, have you thought about what you'd like to be when you are older? We heard about Kaleb wanting to become an architect. What about you? Your drawing is excellent. If you worked at it, you could perhaps become an artist.'

'I want to be like Mummy and join the police,' said Jude.

'I suppose the police need artists, too,' said Fliss, laughing. 'No, I'm not making fun of you, Jude. It's great that you've got something you are aiming for. I've always found that really helps when things get difficult. You at least know what direction you want to go in. What about you, Quoia, what do you want to be?'

Quoia laughed. 'That's easy. For as long as I can remember I've wanted to be a doctor, like Daddy. The idea of caring for people and making them better has always seemed like the best and most important job in the world. The arrival of coronavirus just makes me think I've been right all along.'

CHAPTER TEN

SATURDAY THE 4TH OF APRIL 2020

The children were very quiet at breakfast.

'Come on, everyone,' said Fliss. 'I know you were upset last night because Mummy and Daddy were both at work and couldn't share a Skype call with you. But you shouldn't let it spoil your day. Most importantly, as I said last night, you shouldn't let them know how disappointed you are if you exchange texts or other messages with them. I'm sure they've got more than enough to cope with right now. The last thing you want to do is add to their worries and make their lives more difficult than they already are.'

'I know you're right,' said Quoia. 'I'm sure we all do. But it was such a disappointment when we'd been looking forward to talking to at least one of them.'

'Yes, I understand. It's the same for me. You'd not believe how much I worry about Belinda and Michael with things as they are. They each phone me every few days but part of me just wishes they could be here with us while all this is going on in the world.'

'You wouldn't have room for everyone,' said Jude.

Fliss smiled. 'Yes, Jude, I know. But that doesn't stop me wishing.'

'Daddy said Belinda is an army officer in England and Michael's in Canada,' said Quoia. 'I can see why you're as worried about them as we are about Mummy and Daddy.'

'Belinda's been helping build that big new hospital that they opened in London yesterday for coronavirus patients. I spoke to her last night and she sounded exhausted.'

'What does Michael do?'

'He studied journalism at university. He worked in Edinburgh for a while afterwards. He's been in Canada for the past two years, working on a newspaper in Vancouver, which is over on the west side of the country. He intended to come back to Scotland last year but met someone. By coincidence, his name is also Michael and he works on the same newspaper. They moved into an apartment together last year. I was due to travel over in May, that's next month now, to Vancouver to see that part of the country and meet this other Michael. The idea was for me to stay for three weeks. Obviously, that's not going to happen. I just hope it will be possible sometime later in the year.'

Kaleb thought Fliss was going to cry.

Quoia walked over to her aunt and gave her a hug. 'Are you all right, Fliss?'

Thank you, Quoia. I'll be fine. Things have been difficult, but I've been much less lonely since the three of you arrived. I'm grateful for the company. You take my mind off things I'd worry about. Having you here is a huge help to me, especially with the world in chaos.'

'We're all really grateful you could have us stay,' said Quoia 'I know that's true for Mummy and Daddy too.'

'Look,' said Fliss, 'let's talk about what we're going to do today. It seems to me that the routine we've got into over the last couple of mornings has worked quite well.' Fliss held up her hand as Jude started to say something. 'Yes, I know it's a Saturday, Jude, but a couple of hours' schoolwork will help you all keep up and then we can do some more art before lunch.'

'Can we go and look at the stable block beyond the ruined house on our walk this afternoon, Fliss?' asked Jude.

'Yes, it looks like it's going to be a nice day. Less cloud than yesterday and more like Wednesday and Thursday. It's still due to be fairly chilly, though. We can go to the stables and then take a nice circular walk that follows a path through a cleared forest back to the Pineapple.'

Things were going to plan until they were eating their lunch of sausages and mashed potatoes. Then Fliss's phone rang. She'd left it on a worktop in the kitchen.

After she picked it up, she looked at the children. 'I'm sorry, it's an old friend and I need to talk to her. I'll take it down to your room, Quoia, so I don't disturb your lunch.'

After Fliss had answered her phone and gone downstairs, the children looked at one another.

'I think it's a call from the person she's got staying in the apartment,' said Jude.

'That really is a silly idea,' said Quoia. 'She stayed with us last night while we were watching *Charlie and the Chocolate Factory.*'

'Yes, but then we all went to bed earlier than on the first two nights. It was like Fliss had somewhere else she wanted to be but didn't want us ringing the apartment doorbell again. I'm right, aren't I Kaleb?'

'I don't know, Jude.'

'You just like living here so much that you refuse to think anything might be wrong.'

'Leave Kaleb alone, Jude,' said Quoia. 'He's right. None of us know.'

They'd finished their lunch and Jude and Kaleb were doing the washing up by the time Fliss returned.

73

'I've put some clingfilm over yours, Fliss,' said Quoia. 'I think it's still quite warm, or I can put it in the microwave for you if you like.'

'I'm really grateful Quoia, but I'm afraid I've got to go out again.'

'You said you'd take us out for a walk!' said Jude.

'I know, I'm sorry. My best friend Judy lives over in Greenock. I've known her since art school. She's an artist who specialises in seascapes and paintings of boats. She lives on her own in a house overlooking the Firth of Clyde. She was married for a while when we were younger, but it didn't work out. Her problem is that she's running extremely low on paints and the usual suppliers aren't open. She says she's even looked on Amazon, but they are saying that during the current crisis non-essential items might be delayed and she thinks that includes artists' paints.

'I got a large delivery of stuff, including the sort of paints she uses, just before the lockdown. I've promised to take some over this afternoon. I'm terribly sorry. I don't want to let you down but there's no-one else who can help her. I know she'd do the same for me if things were the other way round.'

'How long will you be?' asked Quoia.

'It must be more than 50 miles each way, including crossing Glasgow on the M8. On a normal Saturday afternoon there would be queues on the motorway through the city. I simply don't know what it will be like today. The roads might be empty. But it's going to be a couple of hours or more for the round trip.'

'Could we come with you, Fliss?' asked Kaleb.

'I'm sorry, no. I suppose it's arguable that I'm making a delivery necessary for her to do her work from home. But I still think that this is probably outwith the lockdown rules. I'll attract much less attention if I go by myself.'

'Are you saying that you want us to stay here on our own?' asked Jude.

'To be fair, Jude, it won't be all day. I know you are all sensible and can be trusted.'

'Well in that case, can we be trusted to go out for a walk on our own? If we don't, we might miss going for a walk at all today and we are supposed to exercise.'

Fliss smiled. 'I think you've got me there, Jude. Yes, the three of you can go for a walk on your own. But there must be some rules. The first is that you stick together the whole time you are out. The second is that you don't go to the ruined house or stables, just to the Pineapple. And the third is that you two boys must do exactly what Quoia tells you. The last rule is that you take great care crossing the main road. I'll give you the spare front door key Quoia. Before I go, I'll also check you know how to set the burglar alarm, and un-set it, of course. Incidentally, for my part I promise I'll stick to social distancing rules. I'll just drop the paints off and come straight home.'

'You showed me the alarm yesterday, Fliss,' said Quoia. 'I'm sure I'll have no problem. Can we help you carry any paints down to your car?'

'No, that's fine, thanks. I keep my reserve stocks in the garage. I'll pick some up on my way to the car.'

Fliss went downstairs with the remains of her lunch still uneaten.

'I think we should see her off, again,' said Jude. 'Let's check if anyone else is going with her.'

'Oh, all right,' said Quoia, sighing.

Kaleb reluctantly followed the other two out onto the balcony. Jude had been right. If Fliss was keeping someone else in the apartment, then Kaleb didn't want to know about it. He really did prefer living here to living in Kirkliston, though he wished that Mummy and Daddy could be here too.

The children were standing at the far end of the balcony, overlooking the drive, when Fliss came out through the gate between the back corner of the house and the front corner of the garage.

She smiled when she saw them, then called up, 'Remember what I said about the rules while you're out.'

'We will, Fliss,' called out Jude, to Kaleb's surprise.

Fliss was carrying two Sainsbury's plastic shopping bags as well as her handbag, which was slung over her shoulder. She walked round the car and then put one of the bags down on the drive as she opened the tailgate. It fell over and Kaleb could see what looked to be boxes of paints like some he'd seen in the studio.

Before getting into her car, Fliss waved, then she started it and reversed onto the lane before driving off towards the village.

'There were certainly boxes of paints in the bags,' said Quoia. 'And I don't think there was time for anyone to get into the car and hide from our view before we got to the end of the balcony. Are you happy, now, Jude?'

'Maybe she left them in the apartment,' said Jude.

'That's silly,' said Quoia. 'Look, from here you can see in through the apartment's big front windows. If there was anyone there, we'd see them.'

'Not if they were standing close to the wall on this side,' said Jude. 'And there must be a bathroom at the back that we can't see into.'

'I give up!' said Quoia. 'Look, are we going for a walk, or aren't we? If we are, then let's get ready. I'll put some water and biscuits or sweets in that small pack of Fliss's.'

*

While they were walking along the street past the near side of the village green, Kaleb saw the girl again, in the cottage window. This time when he waved, she waved back. He was following Quoia and Jude, so neither of them saw the exchange and he said nothing about it.

No-one said anything at all until they were walking along the track that ran through the avenue of Redwoods.

'Did you two believe Fliss about the artist friend and the paints?' asked Jude.

'She did have paints in that shopping bag,' said Kaleb.

'I know, but we've been in lockdown for a couple of weeks now, even though it feels like forever. Surely if this friend, Judy, had needed paints so badly, she'd have been able to get hold of some before now. To ring Fliss at lunchtime on a Saturday because she's suddenly run out seems really odd.'

'Can we change the subject, Jude?' asked Quoia. 'Fliss took us in when she didn't need to and she's doing a huge amount for us. It doesn't feel right to be looking to find fault with her.'

'I bet you think the same as Quoia, don't you, Kaleb?'

'Yes, I do, Jude. I like Fliss and I like the house.'

'Maybe when all this is over, we could leave you here. It would give us more room back in Kirkliston.'

Quoia stopped walking and turned to face her brothers. 'Please, Jude, stop it. You're just looking for reasons to argue. Let's enjoy our walk.'

The three of them walked in silence again until they reached the gates of the walled garden.

'They're open!' said Kaleb. 'We can go in.'

Quoia looked around. 'There's still a sign on the gate saying the garden is closed. But it's obviously not, not right now, anyway. If anyone tells us to leave, we must, but let's at least go and look at the Pineapple from this side while we can.'

Kaleb set off at a run through the orchard and up the slope towards the Pineapple. He realised that Jude was catching him up and ran as hard as he could. At the last minute, Jude slowed down, leaving Kaleb to get to the base of the Pineapple first. Kaleb knew Jude was a faster runner and was extremely competitive. It was unusual for him to let Kaleb beat him at any sport.

The ground floor of the central part of the building had an open front. This was formed by four round columns with an arch between the tops of the central two. There were carvings above the arch, some ornate lettering and a what looked like a flower on a heart over a piece of rope. Above them was a motto, FIDELIS IN ADVERSIS. Inside the building, beyond the columns, was a small enclosed area with an ornate door in the rear wall and a plainer door on each side wall. There was also an information panel on one side.

Quoia caught up with them. 'Remember not to touch anything.'

Kaleb walked a little way down the slope and turned round, so he could admire the spectacular upper parts of the Pineapple itself. He couldn't believe how complicated the stonework was. The result really did look like a huge pineapple.

Jude and Quoia walked down to join him. It didn't take Jude long to get bored. 'Can we head back now?'

'Let's have some water and something to eat, first,' said

Quoia. 'Here, give me the pack, Jude. Hang on, what's this? I said to leave the torches back at the house. You've been carrying more than you need to. Do you want a biscuit, Kaleb?'

They all had something to eat and drank some water. Then they set off back through the orchard towards the gates.

CHAPTER ELEVEN

They were close to the entrance to the walled garden when the same girl and boy they'd seen the previous day appeared in the gateway. The children walked across the grass to meet Quoia, Jude and Kaleb. The boy was dressed the same as before, but the girl had on a blue jumper and jeans. They stopped a safe distance from the three children.

'Hello,' said the girl, smiling. 'We saw you walking over this way. There's never anyone to talk to in the village so we thought we'd come and introduce ourselves. I'm Florence Durand and this is my brother Jamie. We live by the village green. You know that already, though, because you waved at me on your way out.' She looked at Kaleb.

'I waved at you on Wednesday, too,' said Kaleb, 'but you didn't wave back.'

He saw Florence and Jamie look at each other and smile.

'We're very pleased to meet you,' said Quoia. 'I'm Sequoia Dalgleish, though people usually call me Quoia. These are my brothers Jude and Kaleb.'

'You've moved into the house by the river, haven't you? The one they built in a field beyond the edge of the village a few years ago.'

'That's right, Florence. We normally live near Edinburgh, but Mummy's in the police and Daddy's a doctor. After our schools closed, they found it hard to look after us and go to work. We've moved in with our Aunt Fliss. She's an artist so she has the time to look after us at home.'

'Have you looked at the Pineapple yet?' asked Jamie. 'You're lucky that the garden is open. It's been closed most of the time since the lockdown, though we know a way in. I think it's open today because they've been mowing the grass.'

'Yes, we were just heading back.'

'OK, then. I'm sure we'll see you around. We're going up to the Pineapple.'

'Bye, then.' After the children made a point of passing one another without getting close, Quoia carried on through the open gateway, with Jude and Kaleb following her.

Suddenly Kaleb heard her gasp and saw her put her hand to her mouth, as if to stifle a scream. At the same time a figure emerged from behind the left-hand wall. It was Florence. But it was another Florence, because when he looked back, he could see Jamie and the first Florence standing and watching, with broad grins on their faces.

Jude laughed. 'They're twins! Fliss said something about another sister. She just didn't say they were twins!'

'You really frightened me,' said Quoia to the second girl.

'I'm sorry,' the girl said, smiling. 'Well, to be honest, I'm not sorry. I'm Isobella. We thought you might not know there were two of us and that's a trick we sometimes play on people we're meeting for the first time. I'd offer to shake your hand, but I'm sure you'll understand if I don't as we're meant to keep socially distanced.'

Florence and Jamie had walked up behind them, still grinning. They stopped a little way away.

'I have to admit it's a good trick,' said Quoia, before doing the introductions again for Isobella.

'Where are you going now?' asked Isobella.

'We're walking back to the village,' said Quoia.

'Can we walk with you?' asked Florence. 'We'll keep our distance, but we can still all talk. It seems like ages since we've had anyone to talk to apart from one-another and Mum.'

'Where's your dog?' asked Kaleb.

'Oban?' said Jamie. 'We'll be taking him out for a walk later so left him at home this time. We thought if he barked you might hear him and notice us before we wanted you to.'

'We were going to stop off at Elphinstone Tower on the way back,' said Jude. 'You must know the place very well.'

'Hang on, Jude. Fliss told us not to,' said Quoia.

'No, she didn't. I was listening carefully. She only told us not go to the house or the stables.'

'That's true, but she also said we were only to go to the Pineapple. That's why you kept the torches in the pack, isn't it, Jude?'

'But the tower is on the way back from the Pineapple. I'm sure she'd have said if she'd not wanted us to go there.'

Kaleb could see Quoia was in two minds.

Then one of the girls, he didn't know if it was Florence or Isobella, stopped walking. 'Look, if it helps, we have to go straight back because we need to get home before Mum gets back from the supermarket in Stirling. We weren't planning to come out until Florence saw you heading this way. Mum won't be happy if she gets home and finds we've all disappeared.'

'That's settled then,' said Quoia, with obvious relief. 'We'll leave the tower to another day.'

Kaleb was surprised that Jude didn't get angry, but he seemed to be on his best behaviour. Kaleb wondered if he was trying to impress the twins.

'I can't tell you apart,' Jude said. 'It's hard to know which of you is which.'

'I'm sorry,' said one of the twins. 'We don't usually dress alike, but we do have these jumpers and we wanted to surprise you. Look, how would it be if I push my sleeves up? I'm Florence, by the way.'

'Thank you, that would be much less confusing,' said Jude, smiling.

'These big trees are Redwoods, which are also called Sequoias,' said Florence. 'Were you named after the tree, Quoia?'

'No, it was the other way round.' Quoia went on to explain the historical link.

'I like the names Florence and Isobella,' said Jude. 'Are you named after anyone?'

'We're named after our grandmother, our father's mother,' said Isobella. 'Her two first names are Florence Isobella, so we got one each. She lives in Paris. We've not seen her since we visited last year.'

'That must have been nice,' said Quoia.

'Sort of,' said Isobella. 'Mum and Dad split up when we were younger, seven years ago this year. It was nice to see our grand-maman but all the relatives on that side got a little confusing. And Dad's got a new family now, a wife and two young boys. I don't think his wife likes us very much. Dad left Mum to be with her when they were all working for the same company in London, but I think she's jealous of us. It's like she thinks that seeing us will make him want to come back to Mum.'

Florence laughed. 'As if that's likely. She'd never have him back. He left her in a real jam, and I don't think she's ever forgiven him. We were seven and Jamie was only four and it was really hard for her.'

'Our aunt said you moved up here to live with your other grandmother,' said Quoia.

'Ah, I bet she's a member of the bowling club, isn't she?' asked Isobella. 'Mum says they are all a load of gossips.'

'Our Aunt Fliss says the same about them,' said Quoia. 'I think she only joined because she was lonely after our Uncle Jim died.'

'They're right, anyway,' said Isobella. 'We moved up here to gran's cottage the year after Mum and Dad split, when they got divorced. Grandma Lily was a lovely lady. She was 79 when she died last year.'

'I sometimes wish that one of us had been named after her,' said Florence. 'It seems unfair that we were both named after our French grand-maman.'

'Well we know why that was,' said Isobella. 'It's probably better the way things are.'

'Why was that?' asked Jude.

'It's a really long story,' said Isobella. 'Let's just say that although it worked out well enough for our grandmother, Lily is sometimes seen as an unlucky name in our family. Right now, though, we're coming up to the main road. It might not be a good thing for anyone in the village to see six children all together. We've kept our distance as we should, but they'll not know that.'

'You are the ones that need to be back first, before you're missed by your mother,' said Quoia. 'We'll stay back from this side of the main road and finish off our biscuits and sweets. That should give you time to get home before we reach the village green.'

'Can we all meet up again?' asked Jude. 'Florence, you said the three of you had no-one else to talk to in the village. We're the same. Aunt Fliss has got a big garden. I'm sure she'd not mind if you called in so we could all talk. We could do it perfectly safely while keeping our distance from each other.'

Kaleb was surprised to hear Jude suggesting they break the lockdown rules like this. What he said was sensible enough. It just broke the rules and Jude was someone who cared a lot about rules when it suited him. From the look on Quoia's face, Kaleb got the feeling that she was equally surprised by what Jude had said.

'That's a good idea,' said Florence. 'Can you tell me your mobile phone number, Quoia? I'll add you as a contact. Then we can keep in touch by text.'

Quoia told Florence her mobile number and Florence immediately sent her a text, so Quoia also had her number.

'We'll need to talk to our Aunt Fliss, of course,' said Quoia.

'We'll have to talk to Mum, too,' said Isobella. 'But I hope she'll think it's a good idea.'

'Me too,' said Quoia. 'Right, we'll wait here until you're out of sight on the lane.'

*

Kaleb was standing by the large windows at the front of the lounge, looking out over the river, when Fliss's car came along the lane and turned into the drive.

'Fliss is back!' he called. Jude was playing a game on his laptop at the kitchen table and Quoia was at the far end of the studio, looking at a book she'd found on the bookshelves.

Jude stood up.

'You're not going to watch Fliss from the balcony again, are you, Jude?' asked Kaleb.

'No, I suppose that might look odd.'

Fliss looked weary when she came up the stairs to the kitchen.

'Are you OK, Fliss?' asked Quoia.

'I'm fine, thanks, Quoia. I should have finished my lunch before setting off, though. Did you throw away what was left of it?'

'No, it's in the fridge. I can heat it up in the microwave if you like. Did Judy like the paints?'

'What? Oh, yes. She's always been a bit disorganised and she'd let it get to the point where she didn't have enough white left to finish the painting that she's in the middle of. She was extremely grateful. The motorway through Glasgow was very quiet. Everywhere was very quiet, for that matter. There were quite a lot of police about, though. It wasn't a very pleasant journey. Did you all have a good walk?'

'Yes, we did, Fliss,' said Quoia.

'And did you stick to my rules?'

'Completely, though there is something we want to talk to you about later.'

'I'm intrigued. Look, while I eat, does anyone mind if I put some music on? Have you any requests? I've got a fair selection on my phone that I can play over the sound system in here. How about something by Ed Sheeran?'

*

Kaleb had spent the hour before tea practicing his piano in his room while the others were upstairs.

After their tea, the children talked to Daddy on Skype. He said he was expecting Mummy home much later. It was nice to talk to him, but again Daddy seemed tired. They told him about the schoolwork they'd been doing online and about their art classes with Fliss. They also told him about their walks.

Kaleb was surprised that Jude didn't say that Fliss had left the children so she could travel to Greenock, or talk about meeting Florence, Isobella and Jamie. He'd have thought those were the sorts of things Jude would mention. He wondered if Jude realised that their father might object to their plans to meet the Durand children again because it was against the lockdown rules. They did tell him about going to see the broch and the castle the previous day. When he asked, Sequoia assured him it had only been a short drive and they'd all found the walk really interesting.

Again, Kaleb came away from the conversation with his father feeling quite sad. Afterwards, Fliss's phone rang and she went downstairs again to take the call.

When she came back upstairs, she suggested they put another film on. This time it was one the children had brought with them, *Brave*. Kaleb enjoyed it.

Fliss made cheese and biscuits for supper, with some grapes. They sat in the lounge eating, with more music on.

'That was your father who rang earlier. He wasn't happy that we'd driven to see the broch and castle yesterday because he thought that was against the rules. I explained to him that we are a little limited in what we can do from the house and persuaded him that you do need some variety in your exercise. He ended up agreeing it had been the right thing to do. I was surprised that he didn't question my going to Greenock today and leaving you here. I can only assume you didn't tell him and I'm grateful for that. I know it would needlessly have worried him.'

'We didn't think we should,' said Jude. 'Fliss, there's something we need to talk to you about.'

'What is it?'

Jude looked at his sister. 'Quoia, you're better at this than I am. Can you tell Fliss about today?'

Quoia looked at Jude, and then at Fliss. She went on to tell Fliss about their walk to the Pineapple and meeting the other children. The only part she missed out was Jude wanting to go to Elphinstone Tower on the way back.

'Is that it?' asked Fliss. 'I thought you were going to tell me you had broken my rules after all and had been to the ruined house or the stables.'

'No, we did what you said. It's just that we know what we talked about with Florence and Isobella and Jamie would be against the lockdown rules, even though it seems perfectly safe if we keep our distance. We don't want to get you into trouble.'

'You want to meet them in the garden here?'

'That's right. It's well screened so no-one would see. And we'd keep our distance, obviously. It's just that we all got on quite well and it would be nice to get to know them better.'

'As far as I'm concerned that's fine. But it will have to depend on what their mother thinks. I can put out a few garden chairs, and maybe one or two other things, come to think of it. They'll have to bring their own drinks and snacks, because it would be a risk to them to take anything from us. If we clearly say which of the garden chairs are for their use, then we can leave them out for a few days afterwards and let nature kill off any virus. Come to think of it, we can do the same on the balcony. It's accessible using the steps at the far end, so they'd not have to come into the house. There would obviously be some risk, but I'm happy to accept that if their mother is.'

'What we want to do would be against the lockdown rules, wouldn't it, Fliss?' asked Jude.

'Yes, Jude, it would. If we did this, you'd have to make

sure you didn't tell anyone, especially not your mother or father. We'd also need to be sure that no-one saw a group of people who didn't live here on the balcony. Almost nobody uses the lane out there anyway, but if someone came along walking their dog it wouldn't look good. How do you feel about that, Jude?'

Kaleb could see that Jude was having difficulty making his mind up.

'It's something I'd like to do, Fliss,' said Jude.

'Are you sure you are happy with the idea of not telling anyone about it afterwards?'

'Yes, I am.'

'OK, how about you two?'

'Definitely,' said Quoia.

'Me too,' said Kaleb.

'Well tomorrow's Sunday. The weather forecast says it's going to be sunny and the warmest day so far this year. Quoia, I suggest you text Florence and invite them over tomorrow afternoon, after lunch. Say around 2 p.m. Tell her I need to know that their mother is happy with the idea, though.'

CHAPTER TWELVE

SUNDAY THE 5TH OF APRIL 2020

When he lifted the roller blind in his bedroom, Kaleb found himself looking at a cloudless sky. The morning light was coming from his right and it lit the far bank of the River Forth beautifully.

For once, he was dressed and upstairs in the kitchen before Quoia and Jude, though they both came up the stairs before he started on his bowl of Rice Krispies.

Fliss had already eaten her toast. She'd been standing in the lounge window looking at the morning view when he had arrived.

With the children eating their breakfasts, she stood up. 'Right, we need a plan for today.'

'Not more schoolwork, Fliss? Not on a Sunday?'

'No Jude. It seems only fair to have the day off.'

'Yes!' said Jude, fist pumping in a way that Kaleb always found annoying.

'Thank you for asking Florence for her mother's mobile phone number last night, Quoia,' said Fliss. 'After you'd all gone to bed, I had a long conversation with Erica Durand.'

'What did she say?' asked Kaleb.

'Well as you know, Florence had already told Quoia that their mother was happy with them coming over this afternoon. I wanted to talk to her mainly to ask if she wanted to join them. She did, which will be nice. We both thought it was funny that although I've lived here three years, it took your arrival to put the two of us in touch with one another. We ended up talking for much longer than I'd expected.

'The plan is for them to come over at 2 p.m. I was up early this morning and had a look through the side of the garage that I've always used to store stuff I intend to sort through one day. The result was a folding badminton net and poles that Jim and I sometimes used in the garden of our house in Stirling with the children. Even better I found four badminton racquets and two tubes of shuttlecocks.

'My search also unearthed a game of swing-ball that dates back to when the children were younger and a set of plastic boules, as well as four folding garden chairs. I washed everything down and left it on the patio leaning against the side of the garage.'

'We'd have been happy to help,' said Quoia.

'I know you would, but the garage is a real tip and, to be honest, I'd have been embarrassed at your seeing the state it's in, especially after three years' living here.'

'Is that why you always park on the drive rather than in the garage, Fliss?' asked Jude. 'Even though you've got a double garage?'

'That's right, Jude. I'm afraid there was still stuff in boxes when Jim died, which was only a few months after we moved in. I had other things to worry about for a while and I suppose I've simply never got round to sorting it out.'

'I hope it's not brought back sad memories,' said Quoia.

'No, quite the contrary. It brought back some very happy memories from when Belinda and Michael were younger. There are a couple of things you can do for me after breakfast, though.'

'What are they?' asked Quoia.

'We need to find ways of observing social distancing, even if we are breaking the rules by having the Durands visit at all. I've put on the garden table rolls of red and blue electrician's tape I also found in the garage. I want you to put red tape on the handles of two of the badminton racquets and one of the swing-ball bats. I then want you to put blue tape on the remaining racquets and bat. There's some hand sanitiser on the garden table too. I want you to wipe down the handles of the blue-marked equipment, which is all I've touched and all you should touch, using the kitchen roll that's also there and leave everything out to dry. They will be for the Durands to use.'

'What about the boules?' asked Kaleb.

'Good question. It's been years since they were used, long before anyone had heard of coronavirus. I only handled the plastic case. The way to use them is for one of you to open the case and empty out the boules without touching them. Then you only use the red and yellow boules, while the Durand children only use the blue and green boules and, as they are the guests, the jack, which you shouldn't touch at all. The shuttlecocks are in sealed tubes and we can work out later how to mark them, so each side has something to use when they are serving.

'As for the garden chairs, you should use only the artificial rattan sofa and two chairs that are always out on the patio, which we will pull over to one side of the table. After I washed down the folding chairs to remove years of garage dust, I sanitised any parts I touched. They are only to be used by the Durand children and can be set up by them more than two metres from your chairs.'

'Is all this really necessary, Fliss?' asked Jude.

'I suppose that depends on what it's necessary for,' said Fliss. 'In one way, it's probably completely unnecessary as it's unlikely they or you are infected. But the whole point of the lockdown is to avoid taking that chance. By doing it this way, I'm trying to ensure that we've reduced the risk of one group of children infecting the other as far as we possibly can. The thing to remember, though, is that we are breaking the rules by having them here anyway. By taking all these precautions we can at least say we did everything possible to make it safer. Remember, Jude, that you agreed not to mention any of this to your mother or father.'

'Yes, I remember, Fliss.'

'What about Mrs Durand?' asked Quoia. 'Will the two of you be in the garden, too?'

'Ah, I've thought of that. Follow me.'

Fliss led them out onto the balcony, which ran the length of the studio to the far end of the house and was wide enough to house a large round artificial rattan table and four armchairs made of the same material.

'We'll pull two of the chairs on this side of the table and keep the others a little back from the far side. Given how warm it's going to be, I thought Erica and I could sit up here. She can come up the steps at the far end, without touching the handrail of course, and use one of the chairs on the side over there.'

Kaleb realised that the sun, which he'd seen shining from the right from the window of his room immediately below, had moved a little further round, behind the front of the lounge.

'The balcony must be in shadow most of the time,' he said.

'Well spotted, Kaleb. Actually, in summer, the sun is high enough to shine directly onto quite a lot of the balcony, though from behind the house. At this time of year, it will all be, as you say, in shadow. But when it's as warm as it's supposed to be later today, that will be very pleasant.

'I did once pull Jim's leg and say that he'd got the house the wrong way round. I told him it would have been better if we'd found a plot on the north side of the river so the balcony could look over the water and into the sun.'

'What did he say?' asked Kaleb.

'He was quite hurt until he realised that I was joking,' said Fliss. 'To his mind it was much better to have the large windows at the front of the house facing away from the sun, as that made controlling the temperature inside much easier. And the balcony had to be on the front of the house, to enjoy the river views. As he said, it gave us a choice. If we wanted to sit in the sun, we could use the patio behind the house. If we wanted to enjoy a cool drink on a warm evening, then the balcony was perfect. He was right, and I'm grateful that he was able to enjoy the balcony a few times before he died.'

There was a silence after Fliss finished speaking.

'I'm sorry if this is upsetting,' said Quoia.

'It isn't, well not really. The truth is that this afternoon will be the first time that the house has ever really been used the way Jim designed it to be used, with children playing in the garden at the back of the house and adults drinking gin and tonic on the balcony at the front. I'm looking forward to it and I hope Jim will be looking down on us to see it happen.'

Fliss smiled. 'Right, let's get things organised. I talked to Erica about food and drink, and we've got that agreed between us. They're bringing theirs as I suggested, together with their own glasses and anything else they might need. As garden parties go, it will be truly unique. But I'm sure it's going to be really enjoyable, too.'

*

As he went out though the back door from the utility room after lunch, Kaleb looked around. He liked Fliss's garden, just as he liked her house.

There was a path from the utility room back door which led onto a large patio paved, like the path, in slabs of light grey stone. The patio was immediately behind the house. It was sheltered on three sides and had a nice open view out over the garden.

The garden itself was large. Very large by the Kirkliston standards Kaleb was used to. The side of the plot nearest the village was separated from the farmer's field by a dense hedge that looked like it had been there long before the house. Kaleb knew that it continued back across the field. There were two small trees forming part of the hedge, and a large one at the rear corner of the garden. The far end of the garden was marked by a hedge that was much smaller than the one at the side. It had brown leaves that Fliss said would be replaced by green ones in a month or so. She'd told Kaleb that she and Uncle Jim had planted it when they first moved in and that over time it would get taller and denser.

The remaining boundary of the garden, up the outside of the garage and then back to the corner, was formed by a tall wooden fence. Fliss had said she was training climbing plants to grow up the inside of the fence and Kaleb could see traces of them.

Much of the garden beyond the patio was grass, though there were borders with plants on all three sides. There was a rockery in the back-right corner, beyond the garage. There were also some trees that Fliss had said would grow fruit one day clustered in front of the centre of the back hedge.

When Quoia had said how neat the garden looked, Fliss had told her that she had a gardener who came in to help look after everything for a couple of hours each Tuesday.

Kaleb thought how smoothly the preparations had gone. After breakfast, Fliss had insisted that each of them applied some of the factor 50 sunscreen that they'd brought with them from home and wear hats. She'd not been happy that Kaleb only had a baseball cap so had given his ears and the back of his neck an extra layer of protection.

The badminton net had been easy enough to set up. The two upright poles were connected by a metal framework that folded out and had feet that allowed them to stand on the grass.

The swing ball had been more difficult to fix until Fliss had got a large mallet from the garage. Kaleb had offered to help look for it but Fliss was very unhappy about anyone seeing the mess in the garage.

They'd rearranged the furniture on the patio as Fliss had said, leaving the garden chairs for the Durand children to set up when they arrived.

Quoia had looked after marking the badminton racquets and the swing-ball bats with the coloured sticky tape and then sanitising the blue-marked ones for their visitors. She'd then tipped out the boules set on an area of grass not already occupied, without touching any of the boules or the jack.

As he looked round now, Kaleb thought that 2 p.m. couldn't come soon enough.

CHAPTER THIRTEEN

Florence, Isobella, Jamie and their mother arrived a few minutes late.

The girls were first, carrying a picnic hamper between them.

Fliss had used a large rounded stone to prop opened the gate between the front corner of the garage and the back corner of the house and stood back as she welcomed them. Quoia, Jude and Kaleb stood on the patio.

'Hello, you must be Florence and Isobella, though I'm not sure who is who. I'm Fliss.'

'Florence is the one wearing the yellow T-shirt and jeans,' said Isobella, who was wearing a blue T-shirt and denim shorts. 'Mum and Jamie are following. She thought it best if we didn't all walk together as people might wonder what we are doing.'

Jamie arrived a few minutes later, with a lady who Kaleb knew must be their mother, Erica Durand. She seemed about the same age as Mummy, and about her height. She took off her straw sunhat when she said hello to Fliss, to reveal short blonde hair, though she kept her sunglasses on.

'Hello Fliss. It's really odd to be meeting for the first time like this. Perhaps we should do without the kiss on the cheek we might have used a month or two ago?'

'That seems a good idea,' said Fliss, smiling.

Fliss went on to explain the preparations they'd made and how she thought they could keep socially distanced while still enjoying each other's company.

'That sounds good to me. Any questions, children?'

'What if we want to go to the toilet?' asked Jamie.

His mother smiled. 'It's only a five-minute walk back to the cottage. You go there if you need to.' She looked at the Dalgleish children. 'I guess you are Quoia, Jude and Kaleb. I'm happy to meet you. Please call me Erica.'

'Didn't you bring Oban with you, Erica?' asked Kaleb.

'No, we thought he might find it all a bit too exciting and I'm sure he's got no idea at all about social distancing. We'll take him for a walk later.'

Kaleb was disappointed.

Erica smiled. 'Do you like dogs, Kaleb?'

'Yes, but Mummy and Daddy have never let us have one.'

'Not all of us want one,' said Jude.

'Hang on, boys,' said Fliss. 'I think that's a discussion for when this is all over and something like normality returns. Where do you want to put what you've brought with you, Erica?'

'We've had lunch, but there are some snacks and some glasses in the picnic hamper. The large cool box I've brought with me has some cold soft drinks, which I think will be needed by my three. The small cool box that Jamie's carried over has two bottles of very cold sparkling wine in it. I'm sure we can find a way of me pouring you a drink or two without touching your glass. I know you had in mind gin and tonic, but making drinks from two different bottles, with lemon and ice, seemed too complicated. Is that OK?'

'That sounds lovely, Erica. My three can get their drinks and snacks by popping in the back door along there and up to the kitchen. There's an umbrella that goes with the patio table, I'll put that up and it should give shade to help keep your soft drinks and snacks cool.'

After Fliss and Erica had gone up the stairs at the side of the house that led to the balcony, taking the small cool box and a glass for Erica with them, the children stood around for a few moments, not really saying very much.

Kaleb felt very awkward. He was the youngest here and while meeting the Durand children in the walled garden, and then talking to them on the walk back, had felt very natural, this very odd garden party was uncomfortable.

It was Quoia who broke the ice, suggesting a game of boules. She and Jude played as one team, with Florence and Isobella as the other. Jamie got one of the folding chairs and set it up. Kaleb sat on one of the rattan chairs on the other side of the table. He wasn't sure what to say to Jamie but felt he should say something.

As he watched the game of boules, Kaleb realised that the others also seemed uncomfortable. Part of it seemed to be the need to keep social distancing in their minds while playing a game designed to bring people together not keep them apart. But he thought part of it was that everyone else found the circumstances very odd, too.

Even Jude, who usually had no difficulty talking to people, seemed to be tongue-tied. After a short while the boules players appeared to relax a little, but Kaleb realised that he'd still not spoken to Jamie since they'd sat down.

Suddenly he noticed that the perfect blue sky beyond the bottom of the garden had been blemished by a white line moving from left to right. He'd seen it as it emerged from behind the tree in the corner and watched as it progressed very slowly across the sky.

'Look, Jamie, there's a condensation trail up there. We've seen so few aeroplanes recently it looks strange to see one now.'

Jamie looked round so he could see it too. He didn't reply at first. Instead he took his mobile phone out of his pocket and looked at it.

After a couple of minutes, he said, 'It's going from Frankfurt in Germany to Dallas in the United States. It's an American Airlines Boeing 777 and it's flying at 34,000 feet.'

'How do you know that?'

'I've got an app on my phone called Flightradar24. It picks up information from most aeroplanes that are flying around and makes it available on a map. That aeroplane is quite a long way to the south-west of us, but you can still see it because it's so high.'

'Oh, wow, can I look?' Then Kaleb felt a surge of disappointment. 'No, of course I can't. I'll talk to Fliss later about getting it on my phone.'

'You do have to pay for the app, but I don't think it's much. I love aeroplanes and think it's really cool to be able to find out where they are going to and where they've come from when you see them. Like you say, there aren't many flying now because of coronavirus, but normally it's great.'

Kaleb knew far more about Star Wars than he knew about aeroplanes, but he found it fun to ask Jamie questions about them. Jamie said his mother sometimes took him to the back of Edinburgh Airport to watch them taking off and landing, and he found that really exciting. Once, when he was very young, the year before they'd moved to stay with their gran for good, his mum had taken him and the girls to an air show in Fife. He could still remember it as one of the best things he'd ever done. That had been the last time they'd held the air show, though, because the RAF base it was on had closed.

They went on to talk about the Harry Potter books and films, which, from a chance remark by Jamie about Quidditch, they found they both loved.

The boules players had also started chatting much more. Kaleb could see that Jude was trying to show off to Florence and Isobella. Not so much that it was starting to annoy people, not yet anyway.

When the boules players got bored, Jude came over and asked Jamie if he wanted to play badminton. Quoia sat next to Kaleb, who went to get lemonades for them both from the kitchen. When he got back, Florence was setting up a second folding chair on the other side of the table and Isobella was pouring the two of them drinks.

'How do you like Dunmore?' asked Isobella.

'It's nice,' said Quoia. 'Aunt Fliss has been really great to take us in and spends a lot of time with us. The house is wonderful. We normally live in Kirkliston, on this side of Edinburgh. We've got more bedrooms at home there, but other than that, Aunt Fliss's house is better in every way. We couldn't do this at home, for example. Not without people in the houses at the back being able to look at us and people at the sides hearing us.'

Kaleb put his lemonade down. 'What I like best is that Aunt Fliss's house is different enough to deserve a name of its own. It's called Forthview House because of the wonderful views from the front. I also like the idea that it was designed by our Uncle Jim for the two of them to live in.'

'You aunt lives on her own now, doesn't she?' asked Florence.

'Yes,' said Quoia. 'Uncle Jim died not long after they moved in. She's told us the house reminds her of him and I think she gets lonely here sometimes. Of the three of us, Kaleb's the one who is most enthusiastic about the house because he wants to be an architect when he's older.'

'You must have found the Pineapple really interesting then, Kaleb,' said Isobella.

'I did. I've never seen anything like it. I'd love to know how they managed to carve stone so that it all fitted together to make the top of the Pineapple. Dunmore is much more interesting than Kirkliston for its buildings. That's got a really nice church with a lot of history. But there's nothing like the Pineapple.'

'Jude wanted to go to Elphinstone Tower yesterday,' said Isobella. 'Have you visited it since you arrived?'

'Yes, Fliss took us on Thursday,' said Quoia. 'I thought it was really sad that so little was left and a place that had been used to bury people was now open and in such a poor state.'

'How about the big old house itself?' asked Florence. 'Have you seen that yet?'

'Yes,' said Quoia, 'Fliss took us on a tour of the basement level and we looked at the wine cellars. Then we came out the back again and went round to have a look at the ground floor of the main parts of the house, those that are still there.'

'What did you think?'

'I thought it was an amazing place,' said Kaleb. 'But it left me feeling sad, like the tower made Quoia feel. I could imagine so much happening there, but now it's just big walls and a few floors and lots and lots and lots of trees.'

Kaleb saw Florence and Isobella exchange a look, as if deciding whether to talk more.

'Our family's got close links with the house,' said Isobella.

'Are you related to the people that owned it, the Earls of Dunmore?' asked Quoia. 'Fliss told us the story of the place and I've spent quiet a lot of time since our visit looking for more information on the Internet and in the architecture books that belonged to our Uncle Jim.'

Isobella laughed. 'No, hardly! But there are still close links if you go back a bit. I told you about Grandma Lily and how lovely she was. She was quite ill for a while, though she stayed at home. A few months before she died, she started telling Florence and I about the family history.'

'That must have been amazing,' said Quoia.

'It was, but she was careful because she didn't want Mum knowing she was telling us.'

'Why not?' asked Kaleb.

'As far as we can tell, it was because she'd tried to talk to Mum about it when she was younger, and Mum had simply laughed it off. She'd just not been interested. It seemed to me that Grandma Lily was still very hurt about that, all those years later.'

'That's what I thought too, said Florence. 'The thing you need to know is that Mum has two older brothers who moved away many years ago. She keeps in touch, and they sometimes visited Grandma Lily. In our family, and by that, I mean Mum's side of the family, everything revolves around the women. The cottage we live in, for example, has passed down from mother to daughter for generations.

'The same is true of the family stories. The problem was that with Mum not interested, Grandma Lily couldn't tell anyone until she decided we were old enough or perhaps that she was so ill she needed to tell someone while she still could. We've never really talked to Mum about what Grandma Lily told us because she simply brushes aside anything to do with the family as if it's unimportant. To be fair to her, she is often very busy.'

'What does your Mum do?' asked Kaleb.

Florence sat back in the folding chair. 'When we were in London, she worked in a big company buying and selling stocks and shares. It's where she met Dad, and where he later met Daphne, the lady he's now married to in Paris. Mum and Daphne were good friends, though they certainly aren't now. After we moved to Dunmore, Mum set up a public relations company in Edinburgh with a friend she'd been at university with. I think it was doing quite well until the coronavirus arrived. I'm not sure she's so confident about it now. She works from home most of the time, trying to keep the business going, though she has to go into Edinburgh to check for mail at the office once or twice each week.'

'What did your grandmother tell you about the family story?' asked Quoia.

Kaleb saw another look pass between the twin sisters.

It was Isobella who replied. 'I think it would take much longer than the rest of this afternoon to tell you it all. But it seems generations of our family worked at the house or on the estate from not long after it was built for nearly 60 years. That was why one of our ancestors was given the cottage Mum now owns in 1887. Previously it had been part of the Dunmore Park estate.'

'That's amazing,' said Quoia. 'I've found some really good stuff about the house online. There was a film taken from a drone that gives a fantastic impression of the house, though it seems to be a few years old. I also found a photograph taken from directly above that seems rather more recent.'

'I think I know the one you mean,' said Isobella. 'That's the photograph that gave us our name for the house.'

'What's that?' asked Kaleb.

'We call it "The House With 46 Chimneys",' said Florence.

'Is that how many chimneys it had?'

'No, Kaleb, but that is how many it has now. We got the vertical picture on my laptop and placed a red blob on every chimney we could see. Then we counted them, and the result was 46. There would have been more originally, but some were lost when they demolished parts of the north and west ranges in 1972. "The House With More Than 46 Chimneys" just doesn't sound as good.' Florence laughed.

Kaleb looked over to where Jude and Jamie still showed no signs of tiring of their long game of badminton. He'd liked Jamie but wasn't surprised to find Jude got on better with him. They seemed to share a love of competition. It wasn't that Kaleb was bad at competitive games, it was just that he sometimes got bored with them or just couldn't see the point.

He realised that Quoia was speaking again.

'One thing I can't find anywhere, in the books Fliss has, or online, is any reference to the house being haunted. I asked Fliss but she's never heard anything about it. Do either of you know?'

This time it seemed to Kaleb that the twins looked at one another for much longer.

'Why do you ask?' said Isobella.

Quoia had obviously also sensed that her question had disturbed the twins. 'Well, it's nothing really. It's just that there was one part of the ruins where Jude found some steps, near where what's left of the north range meets the east range. I found the place really scary, like I had to get away as fast as I could. Not far away I felt fine, once I'd stopped shaking. Kaleb also felt something there.'

'I just felt unhappy and afraid in that one place,' said Kaleb. 'But Fliss and Jude didn't seem to feel anything at all. And I had no problem anywhere else in the house.'

There was another long pause.

Again, it was Isobella who spoke first. 'That's really interesting. There is a ghost story in part of the family history that Grandma Lily passed to us but, like you, we've never been able to find out anything else about it.'

'We've often been to the ruins of the house,' said Florence. 'Sometimes we've tried to imagine how it must have been in the past. Sometimes, if we can go without Jamie, we've been to see if we can sense anything that connected to the story that Grandma Lily told us. We never have.

'The problem is that if we took Jamie, he'd just laugh at the idea of a ghost. We've not told him anything about the family history, not even as much as we've told the two of you. Please don't mention it to him.'

'We won't,' said Quoia, 'or to Jude, who's the same.'

'Look,' said Isobella, 'if the four of us could go to the house together, could you show us where you felt something? I think I know where you mean, but it would really help to have you show us the exact spot.'

This time it was Quoia and Kaleb who exchanged looks and Quoia who spoke. 'We'll help as much as we can, but it was quite scary.'

Kaleb nodded.

'The problem will be finding a time when the four of us can get away without Jamie and Jude,' said Florence.

'What's wrong with now?' asked Quoia.

'What do you mean?' asked Florence.

'Jude and Jamie look like they could play badminton for the rest of the afternoon. How long would it take us to get to the house and back? Less than an hour as we're only going to one place on this side of it. They probably wouldn't even miss us.'

106

'What about Mum and your aunt?' asked Florence.

'Your mum knows that Kaleb likes dogs,' said Quoia. 'Why don't we just ask them if the four of us can take Oban for a walk over to the Pineapple? We can walk through the village separately, then meet beyond the main road when you've collected your dog. I'll go and talk to Fliss and one of you can talk to your mum.'

'I'll come with you,' said Isobella. 'Well not "with" you, obviously, I'll keep my distance on the steps and the balcony.'

The girls were back in a few minutes.

'What did they say?' asked Florence.

'I think they're enjoying the wine,' said Isobella. 'Mum thought it would be a good idea to get Oban's walk done now rather than have to do it later.'

Quoia grinned. 'The best thing is that we didn't get as far as talking about the Pineapple before they both said what a good idea it was. It means no-one's told us not to go to the house. So long as we don't say anything afterwards, they'll never know we've been.'

'Should we tell Jamie and Jude we're going out?' asked Florence.

'No, let's just go,' said Isobella. 'If they wanted to come too, that would spoil the whole thing. If they miss us, they'll just ask Mum or Fliss where we are.'

CHAPTER FOURTEEN

Florence and Isobella slipped out of the gate between the house and the garage. Then Quoia and Kaleb went into the house through the utility room to collect their boots. Quoia knew where the spare front door key was, so after she'd quickly changed out of the summer dress she'd been wearing into jeans, they went out that way.

They sat on the front steps to put their boots on, then let themselves out of the gate in the front wall. As they closed the gate, Kaleb looked round to see Fliss and Erica in conversation on the balcony.

'Bye, Fliss, see you soon,' he called out, and waved.

After a moment, both Fliss and Erica waved and then returned to their conversation.

Once they were out of sight, Kaleb heard Quoia let out a deep breath.

'That's a relief,' she said. 'I thought Fliss might ask why I'd changed out of my dress. I don't want to get it caught on a branch and ruined. And I want something to protect my legs from the nettles. Are you OK about visiting "The House With 46 Chimneys" again, Kaleb?' She laughed.

'It is a good name for the place, isn't it?' said Kaleb. 'Yes, I'm happy going again if you are.'

They met Florence and Isobella, and Oban, on the track beyond the main road. Oban was on a lead held by Isobella and seemed pleased to see them.

'I see you thought about the nettles too, Quoia,' said Isobella, who Kaleb realised had changed from shorts into jeans.

'We probably shouldn't be too long,' said Quoia. 'We also need to work out how to keep our distance with Oban wanting to say hello to everyone.'

'Does that mean I can't stroke him?' asked Kaleb.

'I'm afraid it does,' said Isobella. She saw the look on Kaleb's face. 'When all this is over and we get our lives back, I promise you can come and pet him as much as you want. He'll love that.'

They turned right at the T-junction of tracks and walked alongside the wood that separated the track from the rear of the ruined house.

'Can I ask why this is so important to the two of you?' asked Quoia. 'You said there was a ghost story in the family history. Can you tell us anything more, and why it means we need to visit the house now?'

'I'm sorry, Quoia,' said Florence. 'Would you mind if we didn't say any more about it for now? Isobella and I talked about it when we were getting Oban and we think it's best if you don't know the details of the story before telling us if you feel anything on this visit. We're concerned that anything we say might influence your reactions when you get to the house.'

'You're beginning to make this seem a little scary.'

'I'm sure we'll be fine,' said Isobella. 'It's a beautiful day and the sun is shining. Nothing could be less spooky.'

'It wasn't nearly this warm, but it was still a nice day when we visited on Thursday and that didn't stop us feeling something that frightened us,' said Quoia.

Isobella had stopped walking. 'Hang on a minute.

Sometimes I wish that Oban wouldn't see it as his duty to sniff every tree we pass!'

Kaleb watched as the dog was gently persuaded to leave his latest tree and move on.

They turned off the track at what Kaleb thought was the same place Fliss had used on their walk to the house. Once in the wood he got the sense that Florence, who was leading, was taking a slightly different route. Not that it made any difference, because they emerged from the wood at the rear of Dunmore Park in the same place as they had with Fliss.

'Right,' said Isobella. 'Can you show us where you both felt something.'

'It was down this ramp that leads into the courtyard,' said Quoia, leading them down.

Kaleb followed, with the twins and Oban a short distance behind him.

'Then we need to go to the left a bit,' Quoia continued. 'To be honest, I was so keen to get back to the ramp that I didn't pay too much attention to where I was. But it wasn't far beyond where we are now, at the rear of the standing part of this range.'

'It's over here,' called Kaleb, who had moved past his sister. 'I've found the steps.'

He'd not really paid that much attention to the steps themselves on their last visit. He'd been thinking about what Jude was doing and how Quoia was reacting. Now he looked, there didn't seem to be anything that made this part of the ruined old house seem any different to the rest of it.

He was looking into a stone alcove that rose to the tops of the walls high above. The two side walls of the alcove were perhaps, by coincidence, the safe social distance of two metres apart, or perhaps a little more. The alcove stretched back maybe three or four metres from where he stood.

Against its right-hand wall was the start of a flight of stone steps. There were five straight steps and the sixth was angled so it started a turn to the left at the back wall. There were four more steps above that one. Each of these carried on with the turn, so that anyone climbing them today would find themselves, at the top of the tenth step, having turned right around so they were facing out of the alcove rather than into it.

There were no more steps above that one. It seemed to Kaleb that they must once have continued, perhaps doubling back on themselves like the few that remained, up to the top of the house. There were what appeared to be several more steps left where they had fallen on the floor, covered in moss. The rest of the floor of the alcove was covered in a scatter of smaller rubble. Grass, ferns and plants were growing up through it and from the edges of the steps that remained, where they met the walls.

Ahead of him, on the left, a rectangular opening framed the space beneath the top few remaining steps. This was empty apart from the sort of rubble on the floor that lay everywhere else. The back wall was black, as if coal had been stored here or someone in more recent times had lit a fire beneath the steps. Parts of the alcove and steps were brightly lit by the sun coming in through gaps in the ruin behind him, though the outer edges of the stairs were in very dark shadow.

Kaleb thought about how he'd felt the first time he'd been here. He got an echo of that same feeling now, of fear and sadness. But it was hard to know if it was real, or just a memory from his previous visit. Except that the more he thought about it, the more real it seemed to be.

'You're going to have to move, Kaleb so we can see,' said

Isobella, from the doorway to his left. 'If we stand beside you, we'll be too close.'

'Oh, yes, sorry.' Kaleb moved away from the steps, through a doorway behind him.

This gave the twins space in the alcove but still allowed him to see the steps. As soon as they came through the doorway, Oban started to bark and to growl at the steps. Kaleb saw the hair on the back of the dog's neck rise. Isobella had him on a short lead but still struggled to control him as he pulled against her. Then his tone changed. He started whimpering and pulling the other way, back towards the doorway they'd entered by.

'You've got to get him out of here, Isobella!' said Florence.

Isobella bent down and scooped Oban up in her arms and then went back out the way they'd entered. Kaleb heard the dog's whimpering get quieter, then stop.

'Where's Quoia?' he asked.

'I don't know,' said Florence. 'She was behind us when you came through into here. I've not seen her since. If she's reacted half as badly as Oban to this part of the house, then I imagine she's retreated with Isobella.'

'Can't you feel anything?' asked Kaleb.

'I just feel puzzled. And I feel frustrated that I don't seem to be able to sense anything else, even though there must be something here to feel. I've never seen Oban react like that to anything except a large and aggressive dog. What about you, Kaleb? You said you felt something the last time you were here.'

'It's the same now. Before you two came in with Oban it was a very mild feeling but getting more noticeable. Look at me now.' Kaleb held out his arms. His forearms were covered in goosebumps and all the hairs on them were standing up.

'It's the same on the back of my neck, just like with Oban.'

'But you're still here,' said Florence. 'Aren't you scared?'

'I am, but I'm also curious. I can feel the fear and the sadness, like last time, but they aren't so strong they force me to leave. But they have been getting stronger the whole time I've been in here and I would like to leave now.'

'OK,' said Florence. 'You go out to join the others. I'll stay here for a couple of minutes to see if I can feel anything when I'm on my own.'

By now Kaleb was moving from foot to foot and back in his anxiety to be away from the alcove and the steps. 'I really don't think that's a good idea, Florence. I think you should come with me.'

'Don't be silly, Kaleb. I'll be fine. Go on, just go!'

Kaleb knew he shouldn't leave Florence on her own in this place, but he couldn't help himself.

He found Quoia and Isobella at the top of the ramp leading back up to the woods. Isobella was still holding a forlorn-looking Oban in her arms and when Quoia looked at him, Kaleb saw her face was completely white.

'Where's Florence?' said Isobella.

Kaleb looked back towards where the staircase was.

'Is she on her own in there?'

Kaleb nodded.

'Here, take Oban.' She walked towards Kaleb and held out the subdued dog to him.

'What about social distancing?' he asked.

'To hell with social distancing! My sister's in there on her own.' Isobella bundled Oban into Kaleb's arms, then ran down the ramp.

'Are you all right, Quoia?' asked Kaleb.

'I was when I got back up here. But for me the horrible

feeling of that place was even worse this time. And that was before I got anywhere near the steps or even the room that they are in. What about you?'

'I was fine at first, but it got worse and worse. Do you think Florence is going to be all right? She told me to go because she wanted to be there on her own.'

'I'm sure she'll be fine.'

It was a few anxious minutes later when Kaleb saw the twins coming back up the ramp. By this time Oban had tired of being carried and had returned to his favourite pastime of sniffing nearby trees while Kaleb held his lead.

'How are you, Florence?' he asked.

'I'm fine thank you, Kaleb. I'm disappointed, though, because I so much wanted to feel what the two of you and Oban could feel and I simply couldn't. Even when I was in there on my own there was nothing at all.'

'I couldn't feel anything either,' said Isobella.

'I think perhaps we'd better be getting back to Forthview House,' said Quoia. 'We don't want anyone asking too many questions and we absolutely can't tell anyone about this.'

'You're right,' said Florence, leading the way back into the wood. 'If anyone asks, we took Oban to the walled garden and back.'

Isobella had smiled and thanked Kaleb when she'd taken Oban's lead back from him. Now she followed her sister into the trees.

Very little was said, beyond occasional warnings about patches of nettles or springy tree branches, until they'd turned onto the track leading towards the main road and village.

'Now we've been to your "House With 46 Chimneys",' said Quoia, 'are you going to tell us why we went? You said on the way there that you would.'

'Well, I don't think we quite said that,' said Florence. 'But I do promise you that we will tell you. It's just that Isobella and I need to talk things through first. Anyway, the story we have to tell is going to take much longer than we've got on what's left of the walk back.'

Kaleb could see that Quoia wasn't happy.

They split up before crossing the main road. Florence and Isobella took a fully recovered Oban home before heading back to the garden party.

As far as Kaleb could see from the gate in the wall from the lane, neither Fliss nor Erica had moved since the children had left. They were still talking and there was now a second bottle of wine standing on the table between them. Both returned the children's waves and smiled.

Kaleb got two lemonades from the kitchen while Quoia changed back into her dress. Then they went out into the garden together.

Florence and Isobella came in through the gate between the house and the garage at almost the same moment.

Jamie and Jude were laying a safe distance apart on the grass in the shade of the large tree at the far corner of the garden.

'Where did you all go?' asked Jamie.

'Mum thought it would be better to walk Oban now rather than leave it until later,' said Florence. 'As Kaleb likes dogs, he came along too, with Quoia.'

'Well that's one job we don't have to do,' said Jamie.

'You don't know what you've been missing,' said Jude. 'We've had a great time here.'

*

It was early evening when the Durands headed back to their cottage, two by two, as they had come.

Fliss said the chairs and games equipment should be left where they were in the garden. She and Quoia made a tea of toasted sandwiches and afterwards, once Kaleb and Jude had washed up the dishes, they all had a Skype call with their mother and father.

Kaleb thought his parents seemed less tired and more relaxed and happier than he'd seen them on previous Skype calls. The children told them about spending the afternoon in the garden and no-one mentioned they'd not been on their own. They also didn't mention walking Oban.

Afterwards they watched *Mamma Mia! Here We Go Again.* Kaleb enjoyed singing along to the songs.

After Fliss had read him a bedtime story, Kaleb pulled up his blind and spent some time standing and looking out over the river. He found himself thinking about 'The House With 46 Chimneys' and the stone steps. He didn't find the memory frightening. He just thought the whole thing was odd. He wondered why the twins had been so keen to return to the house with him and Quoia and thought it was a shame they'd not told their story. What could be so important they had to keep it a secret?

CHAPTER FIFTEEN

MONDAY THE 6TH OF APRIL 2020

In Kaleb's mind, the mornings at Forthview House were becoming a pleasant routine.

Jude thought differently. 'But we only had one day off schoolwork at the weekend. It's not fair that we've got to work again this morning!'

'That depends how you think about it, Jude,' said Fliss.

'What do you mean?'

'Well how long are you at school for each day? I mean during normal times, when the world's not been brought to a halt by coronavirus.'

'8.30 a.m. to 3.30 p.m. for four days each week, that's seven hours, and we finish at 1.05 p.m. on Fridays. But that includes lunch on four days each week and breaks every day.'

Kaleb tried to hide his smile with his hand. He thought he knew what Fliss was going to say next.

'There you go, then,' she said. 'Even taking breaks and Friday afternoons off, we'd have to do two hours every morning for perhaps fourteen days each week to keep up.'

'There aren't fourteen days in a week!' There was a pause, then Jude laughed. 'I think you've got me, Fliss. But you should count our art lessons too. And the time we spend learning about the history of the area.'

'I accept that, Jude,' said Fliss, smiling. 'But even so, I'm not being mean when I ask you to do two hours' schoolwork this morning.'

'Hang on, though,' said Jude, 'our Easter holidays should have started on Friday. That means you've got us working in holiday time.'

'And that's the only way I can think of to make up for not working two hours each day for fourteen days a week.'

By now they were all laughing.

'Let me be serious with you for a moment, Jude,' said Fliss. 'If we didn't do schoolwork for two hours each morning, how would you spend that time?'

'I don't know. I'm sure I'd think of something.'

'One day, hopefully sooner rather than later, this coronavirus crisis is going to come to an end. When it does, I think a lot of people, adults and children, are going to find it hard to readjust to the "normal" world again. I used to be a teacher. It wasn't so obvious in my subject, art and design, but it seemed to me that in many subjects, once a child started to fall behind then it quickly became exceedingly difficult to help them catch up again.

'I've promised Henry and Anna that I'll look after you to the best of my ability. To my mind that includes doing what I can to make sure you do everything possible to keep up with schoolwork. I owe it to them to do that. Mostly, though, I owe it to the three of you. So even though it would be the school holidays in normal times, I think we should spend two hours most mornings, especially in the week, on schoolwork. Are you prepared to go along with me on that, Jude?'

'Yes, Fliss. Can we do art, afterwards?'

'If you all want, we can do it later,' said Fliss. 'I need to go shopping today and before lunch seems the best time. I'd forgotten what it's like to feed so many mouths and we need to stock up.'

'Can we come with you, Fliss?' asked Jude.

'It might not be a nice experience,' said Fliss. 'There may be a queue outside Sainsbury's, like there was when I went on Thursday. And the inside of a supermarket's a fairly stressful place at the moment.'

'We could help, Fliss,' said Quoia.

Fliss was quiet for a moment.

'I tell you what,' she said. 'I know you've not been far since you arrived here last week. Even Tappoch Broch and Torwood Castle were only a few miles away. I'm prepared to take the three of you with me to Sainsbury's. But you must all do exactly as I say, and only one of you can come into the shop with me. The other two must stay in the car. Does that seem reasonable?'

'Can I come in with you, Fliss?' asked Jude.

'I'll let the three of you decide between you who comes in with me. First, though, I want to see two hours of schoolwork and then we can discuss our shopping list.'

*

The roads in Stirling were extremely quiet.

When they arrived, Fliss reversed into a space that backed onto a hedge some distance from the supermarket itself.

'People are parking fairly sensibly and leaving spaces,' she said, 'but over here, with any luck, no-one will park next to us. That will make loading the car easier afterwards. One of the things with this coronavirus is that it makes activities that you'd never have thought twice about before feel more like military operations, with loads of planning and preparation needed.

'Right, Jude, as you're the one coming in with me, I want

you to be responsible for the shopping list. When we've got something, you can cross it off with this pen. I don't want you to touch anything at all. Not the shopping trolley or any of the shopping or anything else. And you are to be extremely careful about keeping two metres from anyone else in the shop.

'I've got a Sainsbury's app on my phone, so I can scan stuff as I take it off the shelves and put it straight into bags in the trolley. I know where most things are in the shop, which is a bonus. Then I just need to pay with a card at the end. You will also be responsible for the hand sanitiser, Jude. Keep it in your pocket along with these pieces of kitchen roll. I'll use it to clean the handle of a trolley before we go in and then my hands after we come out, and again before I get into the car at the end. Do you have any questions?'

'Are we going to have to queue to get in?' asked Jude.

'It looks like there's a short queue of people, all nicely spaced out, but I don't think it will take us long to get in. Are you ready? Good. Quoia and Kaleb, it goes without saying that you should stay with the car. I've left the key there in the centre console so you can wind down windows if you want. It's another quite nice day and could get warm when the car's in the sun. But watch out for anyone getting too close to the car, especially if the windows are open.'

With that, Fliss got out of the car and Quoia passed her the bundle of shopping bags that had been in the front passenger footwell. Jude got out of the back and walked with Fliss over towards the supermarket.

'I'm pleased Jude was so keen to go with Fliss,' said Quoia. 'I'm not sure I like the idea of going in there very much.'

'I know what you mean,' said Kaleb. 'He thinks we did him a favour by agreeing he should be the one to go. Look, there's a man over at that shopping trolley shelter wiping the handles of the trolleys. It gets quite scary when you see something like that.'

'I suppose it's just a sensible precaution,' said Quoia.

'It makes you think, though. Do you think I did the wrong thing by taking Oban off Isobella when she handed him to me yesterday? I mean, she'd touched him and then I touched him. And I'm sure she would have touched him again later. Isn't that dangerous?'

'You didn't really have much choice at the time. Anyway, you washed your hands when you got back to the house, didn't you?'

'I did,' said Kaleb, 'when I changed out of my boots. But they are saying how important it is not to touch your face with your hands, and I can't be sure I didn't do that after holding Oban.'

'I'm sure it will be fine,' said Quoia.

Kaleb knew she was saying that to make him feel better rather than because she was as sure as she sounded.

There was silence in the car for a while.

'Kaleb, what do you think about what happened at the house? I mean, you've had time to think about it now. How do you feel about it?'

I don't know. At first, after I'd found the steps again, I wasn't sure if I was imagining it, but the feeling just kept on growing. I didn't want to leave Florence alone there, but I was so grateful and relieved when she told me to go.'

'Well for me it was worse yesterday than the first time we went,' said Quoia. 'It also seemed to cover a larger part of the house. Thinking about it stopped me getting to sleep for a while last night. I did wonder at first whether I might have been imagining things, but I think Oban's reaction was all the proof we need that what we felt was totally real.'

'What's odd is the way the twins felt nothing at all. They seemed really disappointed by that, especially Florence.'

'I do wish they'd told us why it was so important to them,' said Quoia. 'I was a little upset on the walk back yesterday because I really believed they were going to tell us about the family history and why we'd gone to the house. But when I asked, well, you were there and heard what they said.'

'I'm sure they will tell us,' said Kaleb.

'If they don't, I'm not going anywhere near the house with them again. It's just too unpleasant to want to repeat without a really good reason.'

They sat for a while in silence.

'From what we can see, the queue to get in is getting longer,' said Kaleb.

'Look,' said Quoia. 'The man in the bright yellow jacket who seems to be managing the queue just spoke to that young couple and they're walking back to their car. I think he was telling them they couldn't go in together as two grownups.'

'I think you're right,' said Kaleb. 'They've driven off. But why wouldn't just one of them go in and the other wait in the car? If they go somewhere else to do their shopping, won't there be the same rules?'

'I'm sure there will. Look, Kaleb, do you think Fliss has thought about how she's going to get the shopping into the car when she gets back?'

'What do you mean?'

'She lives on her own. She's probably used to just putting shopping behind the front seats. But with you and Jude in the back, she's going to have to use the lifting tailgate and she's reversed up to that hedge. If she's not got room to lift up the tailgate it's going to be quite awkward for her.'

'Why don't we see?' asked Kaleb.

Kaleb and Quoia got out of opposite sides of the car and met at the back.

'I think there's room for it to lift without hitting the hedge,' said Kaleb.

'I'm not sure you're right.'

'Let's try then, Quoia.'

Quoia tried to open the tailgate. 'It's locked. Look, there's a button on the key that looks like it's meant to unlock it.' There was a clunk from inside the tailgate. Quoia tried again. 'That's it. You're right Kaleb. It just clears the hedge as it lifts.'

There was a pause. Kaleb was standing to one side.

'Can you reach to close it again, Quoia?'

'Yes, I can. But first you should look at what's inside.'

Kaleb looked. There were some rubber mats on the floor of the luggage space, with a coat and a folded tartan blanket. In the far-left corner, held in position by the blanket pushed up against it, was a Sainsbury's plastic shopping bag.

Quoia leaned into the car and pulled the top of the bag towards her. 'It's the bag of paints she had on Saturday. The one she took to that friend in Greenock.'

'Judy, she was called,' said Kaleb. 'But why is the bag still here? Fliss put two bags in the car, so one's gone. Surely Judy would have needed everything Fliss took?'

Quoia closed the tailgate and the two children got back into the car.

'It's not nice to think that Fliss hasn't been telling us the truth,' said Quoia.

'And that may not be the first time,' said Kaleb. 'Remember her going to deliver a painting that none of us saw?'

'But surely she'd have removed the bag from the car when

she got back?' said Quoia. 'She was up early yesterday, getting stuff ready for the garden party. If she didn't want us to know that the paints were still in the car, she could have moved them then without us seeing.'

'Perhaps she just forgot they were there?' said Kaleb.

'Look, they're coming back. Let's not mention it just now.'

Kaleb watched as Fliss pushed a heavily loaded shopping trolley up to the side of the back of the car. Jude was beside her, talking. Kaleb had a good view from the back seat as Fliss lifted the tailgate and saw a look of surprise on her face.

'Just wait there a moment, Jude.' Fliss leaned into the back of the car and did something, Kaleb wasn't sure what, then stood upright. 'Now, can you pass me the bags, one by one, and I'll put them in the car? Try not to touch the trolley itself.'

Fliss loaded the car, then instructed Jude to use sanitiser on his hands and get in. She then pushed the trolley towards the nearest shelter.

'Jude,' Quoia asked, 'was there anything in the boot before Fliss put the shopping in?'

'Just a coat and some rubber mats on the floor. And a blanket in the corner. There might have been something under the blanket, but I'm not sure. Why?'

'It doesn't matter,' said Quoia. 'We can talk later.'

Kaleb saw Fliss sanitise her own hands and then walk back towards the car.

CHAPTER SIXTEEN

When they returned to Forthview House, Fliss told the children to stay on the drive by the side of car while she opened the front door wide. Then she lifted bags out of the rear of the car and put them on one side for the children to carry upstairs. Kaleb didn't want to show too much interest in what was in the boot as Fliss emptied the shopping, but it did look like she had covered the bag containing the paints with the blanket.

Upstairs, Jude and Kaleb washed their hands before Fliss and Quoia wiped everything down and put it away. Then they too washed their hands.

'I'd been hoping to get some bread flour and yeast,' said Fliss. 'I found a bread maker in its box in the garage when I was sorting out the garden games and thought it would be worth trying. But they didn't have either in stock. Other than that, I think we've got everything we wanted. How do you all feel about sandwiches for lunch and I'll make something hot later?'

While they were eating, Fliss asked what everyone wanted to do in the afternoon. 'The weather's supposed to be much the same as this morning. Pleasant enough with some cloud, but not as warm as yesterday.'

'Will you take us out for a walk, Fliss?' asked Jude. 'On Saturday you talked about going to the ruined stables and then walking through a cleared forest to the Pineapple before coming back here. You couldn't take us then and the stables are somewhere we've not been to.'

'Is that what everyone wants to do?' asked Fliss. 'Good. Let's get the sunscreen on and the hats out. There are plenty of breaks in the cloud and I don't want anyone getting burned. We'll take water, torches and snacks in a pack, like we did when we went to the house.'

'Are we going to have to go back to the ruined house?' asked Quoia.

'Well the track round the wood at the back of the house does end up at the stables if you follow it. But it's a lot shorter to cut through the wood and walk past the house. I don't think we'll go in though, because we've got other things we want to look at.'

Kaleb could see Quoia was relieved not to be going back into the house. He understood how she felt.

*

When they emerged from the wood at the back of the old house, Fliss turned right. She then led them along the path that ran round the ruined part of the north range and outside the west range.

After they passed the grand entrance to the house, they turned onto the start of a broad grassy track that had modern barbed wire fences on both sides. This curved steadily round to the right for a couple of hundred metres until it brought them to the corner of a rather grand building.

'This is the stable block,' said Fliss.

'This corner looks like a child's drawing of a castle,' said Jude. 'Sort of square and with battlements on the top.'

'It does,' said Fliss. 'And you can see the far end of the front of the building has a matching corner. The two little castles are linked by walls with narrow slit windows to the gatehouse in the middle. That carries on the castle theme by having a huge gateway with a slightly pointed arch. It's obvious that when George Murray, the 5th Earl of Dunmore, asked his architect to design this place he told him it had to look like a castle rather than a stable. The architect did a good job. All it needs is a drawbridge and the illusion would be complete.'

'It's a shame it looks so sad,' said Kaleb.

'It is. Those trees growing out of the front and tops of the walls must have been there a long time. And all these growing close to the front wall must be undermining its foundations.'

Jude had walked on while the others stood and looked. 'The gates are partly open. Can we go inside?'

'Stay there until we catch up with you,' said Fliss.

When they got closer Kaleb could see the two half doors stood partly open. They were an odd bluish green colour but were highly decorated and reinforced with large square nails. There were signs on each that were clearly modern additions with white writing on a red background. The gates seemed wide and tall enough to allow a horse-drawn carriage to pass between them and under the arch without a driver sitting on top having to duck.

'The doors look magnificent,' said Quoia. 'But the way they've been left is a bit scary. It's like something out of *Lord of the Rings.* You know, they are open enough to invite you in, but then as soon as you are inside, they slam shut behind you and vicious orcs start swarming everywhere and pouring nasty things from the roof of the passage through there.'

Fliss laughed. 'I know exactly what you mean. I don't think

we'll find any orcs here today, though.'

'The signs don't say you can't go in,' said Jude. They just say that "unauthorised persons enter at own risk". Can we go in, Fliss?'

'Yes, but I'll lead. My memory of this place is that the structure is much more complete than in the house, but there are some dodgy bits of floor where you could fall through. It all feels more real and recent than the house because there's more of it left.'

Fliss led them between the doors and through the broad, high, passage beyond. There were no orcs in sight, thought Kaleb.

The passage led through to a heavily overgrown courtyard. It was difficult to make out detail because of the density of trees growing in parts of it, but they were surrounded on all four sides by ranges of the two-storey building.

'It would be hard to see anything at all if the leaves were fully out on these trees,' said Quoia.

'That's true,' said Fliss. 'The main track through the vegetation leads to the far side of the courtyard.'

Fliss led the way into a large open-fronted space. The ceiling was formed by the bottom of the wooden floor above. In one corner was a brick cylinder, perhaps three metres wide, that reached from floor to ceiling.

'This may be where they kept carriages,' said Fliss.

'I wonder what that's for,' said Kaleb, pointing at the brick cylinder.

'I've no idea,' said Fliss. But the brickwork makes it look much more modern than the rest of the building, which is made of stone. Watch out Jude! That's what I meant by dodgy floors.'

Kaleb saw Jude stop and look down, his foot poised over a

gap where the floorboard had been removed or rotted away.

'Look, let's go back out into the courtyard,' said Fliss.

When they were outside, Kaleb noticed something he'd not seen before, a tubular-framed chair lying on its back in a patch of vegetation.

'Look at that,' he said. 'It looks like someone's just knocked it over and could come back for it at any moment.'

'We should probably get on with the rest of our walk,' said Fliss. 'But let me see if I can find the place that I thought was oddest when I came here with Jim. Yes, there's a path through the undergrowth leading to this corner of the courtyard. There's another of the set of chairs there Kaleb, lying on its side this time. Now look at this. This really faded yellow door has a letter box in it, like it was once someone's front door. It's wide open and if you look beyond you can see that a lot of the interior is still left.' She led the way inside.

'There are even bits of electrical wiring on the stone walls. Look here. This light switch looks quite modern but has been smashed and is now covered in cobwebs. This space beyond the door must once have been some sort of hallway. There's a wooden partition ahead of us which doesn't look as old as the stonework and there's a set of wooden steps with metal edges leading up to the floor above. If you look up, you can see there's not much left of the floor above, so climbing the steps probably isn't a great idea.'

Jude had pushed past Kaleb. He walked over to the bottom of the steps and looked up them. 'Hello! Is anyone at home?'

Kaleb felt the hairs on his arms and neck rise. Then he heard the shrill whinny of a horse in distress. The noise came again, accompanied by some loud banging. It seemed to be coming from beyond a closed wooden door on the right-hand side of what Fliss had called the hallway.

'Jude, come away from those stairs,' said Fliss. 'I've already said you can't climb them.'

The distressed horse whinnied again and then there was silence.

Kaleb had been standing facing the closed door. Now he turned round, to see Jude and Fliss looking at him.

'Did either of you hear anything just then?' he asked.

'I heard Jude call out,' said Fliss, 'was that what you meant?'

'I heard a horse. It seemed to be just beyond this door.'

'I'm sorry, no,' said Fliss. 'It's very quiet in here, I'm sure I'd have noticed that.'

'Me neither,' said Jude. 'Just what Fliss said about not climbing the stairs. Are you all right, Kaleb? You've gone completely white.'

Kaleb still had goosebumps. The thought that what he'd heard so loudly and distinctly hadn't been heard by Jude and Fliss was frightening him.

'I think perhaps we need to get out into the fresh air,' said Fliss. 'Has anyone seen Quoia since we came in here?'

Neither boy had.

Kaleb led the way into the courtyard and then out through the gates. He found Quoia where he expected to find her, on the far side of the clear area in front of the stable block. She looked shaken.

'You too?' she asked.

'I heard a horse. They heard nothing,' said Kaleb.

Fliss and Jude came out between the gates and walked over to join them.

'What is it with you two and old buildings?' asked Jude. 'Every time we're in one you run away.'

'Are you OK?' asked Fliss. 'You both look like you've just

seen a ghost.' She laughed, as if not wanting to sound silly. 'Anyway, does anyone want anything to eat or drink? The path from here runs along the side of the stables and then through the cleared forest area I talked about.'

Kaleb was pleased when they were away from the stables. They'd walked round the outside of the part where he'd heard the horse and he found himself listening intently. He heard nothing, though.

The rest of the walk was very enjoyable. At one point they stopped beside an odd structure standing next to the track. It was about the size of a shipping container but was made of vertical planks of wood. It looked like there were windows or hatches at both ends and a doorway in the middle of the side facing the track. These openings were covered by closed shutters and had wooden awnings overhead, as if to shelter them from the weather.

'What do you think it is?' asked Jude.

'I'm sorry, I've no idea,' said Fliss. 'I do recall seeing it on previous walks. You could almost imagine it serving ice creams on the promenade of a seaside town, but it probably wouldn't be so drab or tatty if that was its role in life.'

A little further on they stood to one side of the track to let a young couple in brightly coloured Lycra clothes pass in the opposite direction on their bicycles. They all exchanged greetings from a safe distance.

Then Fliss directed them off the track and on to a narrow path through dense woods. Kaleb liked this part. It emerged at a corner of what Kaleb realised was the walled garden that housed the Pineapple, at the far end from the gate they'd gone through on their last visit.

'Ah, I'd not thought of this,' said Fliss, using a piece of kitchen roll she'd had in her pocket to try to work the latch on a gate set into a tall brick wall. 'The route normally goes through this gate and into the garden, then past the Pineapple and out of the gate at the far end. I'd forgotten this gate might be locked.'

'So, what do we do now?' asked Jude.

'There seems to be a path along the outside of the garden wall that takes us to the Pineapple. Once we're there, then we can just pick up the route we took to get back last time.'

Fliss was right and they continued their walk back towards the village.

*

Once they were back at Forthview House, Jude and Quoia settled down to carry on with their art, while Kaleb went down to his room to practice on the piano.

Fliss made dinner and after the washing up was done, they were able to speak to Daddy on Skype. He seemed quite happy but said that Mummy was still on duty.

When Kaleb's bedtime arrived, he asked if Quoia could read him a story.

Fliss was happy not to have to and Quoia and Kaleb went downstairs.

'I wanted to talk to you without Jude or Fliss hearing,' he said, after she'd closed his bedroom door and he'd taken off his glasses and put them on his bedside table.

'Yes, me too,' said Quoia. 'Look, have you said anything to Jude about finding the paints in Fliss's car?'

'No, I'm not sure it's a good idea to tell him. He'd just want to tell Daddy that something's not right with Fliss. Quoia, do you think we should do that, tell Daddy?'

'I don't know, Kaleb. It is very odd, but we've not got

anything definite. What can we tell him? That we didn't see her leave with a painting she was meant to be delivering to someone in Stirling and that we found some paints in her car she was meant to have left with a friend in Greenock? He'd be more concerned that she'd been to Greenock than about the paints, and we didn't tell him about that at the time. That would make us seem partly to blame.'

'I know what you mean,' said Kaleb. 'I don't like not telling him, but I agree it would just sound silly.'

'Should I read you something, then? I'm not sure where you've got to in your book.'

'Would you be OK if we talked about the stables instead?' asked Kaleb. 'Did you go into the hallway beyond the yellow door?'

'No. I got close but really didn't like it there. It was like being near the stone steps in the ruined house. I just had to be somewhere else, so turned round and went back out through the gates to where you found me. What about you? You said something about a horse when you came out.'

Kaleb told her what had happened.

'You heard a horse whinny three times and you heard loud banging, yet Fliss and Jude heard nothing at all?'

'That's right,' said Kaleb.

'That's simply weird. And scary.'

'Do you think we should tell Florence and Isobella what happened at the stables?' asked Kaleb. 'You've got Florence's number. You could text her.'

'I'm still not happy they didn't tell us their family story yesterday,' said Quoia. 'I don't think we should mention the stables until they've been open with us.'

'Yes, I see that.'

'Look, the others will be wondering where I am. Can we

skip the reading and just say goodnight?'

After Quoia had gone, Kaleb put his glasses back on and lifted the blind on his bedroom window. He liked looking at the river and the land beyond it in the last of the evening light. This evening, though, he was mostly thinking about what could have frightened a horse enough for it to make the noises he'd heard.

CHAPTER SEVENTEEN

TUESDAY THE 7TH OF APRIL 2020

Kaleb was surprised that Jude settled down to his schoolwork after breakfast without complaint. He realised they'd now been living at Forthview House for long enough to think of this as a normal way to spend the morning. And as he normally did, he used Fliss's computer at the far end of the studio while Quoia and Jude sat with their laptops at the kitchen table.

Fliss talked to each of the children from time to time to discuss what they were doing and how it was going, but she spent most of the two hours working on her commission painting of Sandwood Bay, which Kaleb really liked. The position of the computer meant he was facing away from the rest of the studio most of the time, but he did turn round a few times to see how the painting was progressing.

Afterwards, Fliss set them off on their art projects. Kaleb had finished the drawing of Forthview House as seen from the river, so Fliss took a screenshot on his iPad of a scene from the drone video of Dunmore Park showing the view down onto the ruined house from one side of it. She asked Kaleb to try to draw the old house from that angle in pencil.

Quoia and Jude were both using watercolours. Jude was painting the view out over the river, the one he'd already done in pencil, while Quoia was working from a photograph Fliss had found online of Edinburgh Castle taken from the east end of the Grassmarket.

After about an hour, Kaleb heard Fliss's phone buzz.

She took it out of her handbag and looked at it. 'It's Andrew, the gardener, He's texted to say he's arrived. Did any of you see a white van drive along the lane just now?'

The children shook their heads.

'Neither did I. I suppose that's a sign of being busy and enjoying what we're doing. Anyway, he's parked on the drive and I need to go down to open the gate to the back garden and discuss what I want him to do today. I also need to safely clear off the grass the games stuff that we left out on Sunday.'

Fliss smiled at the children and went downstairs.

'Fliss seems happy that the gardener's arrived,' said Quoia.

'I suppose it means she can get the place looking tidy again,' said Jude. 'You could see on Sunday that the grass had been growing. I guess that's because the weather's been so good.'

A little later, Kaleb heard a lawn mower on the front lawn and Fliss returned to the studio.

She said she was impressed by the progress that Jude had made and offered Kaleb some ideas on getting the perspective right on his drawing, which she said was coming on well. She then went to see how Quoia was getting on.

'Do you like it when the gardener's here?' asked Quoia.

Kaleb saw Fliss turn red.

'What do you mean?' Fliss asked.

'You've not stopped smiling since you got the text from him to say he'd arrived,' said Quoia. 'Well, not until I asked you that question and you blushed. I'm sorry if I've upset you. I shouldn't have said anything.'

'No, it's really not a problem,' said Fliss. 'I'm just a little shocked to learn how transparent I am. The truth is that

Andrew did our garden while we lived in Stirling, so I've known him for quite a long time. He's been a great help to me since Jim died. Then, at about this time last year, his wife died from complications after an operation on her appendix. He's about my age and their two sons moved away a few years ago. We've got to know each other quite well since then.'

'Does that mean he's your boyfriend?' asked Jude.

Fliss smiled. 'I think we're a little old to be thought of as boyfriend and girlfriend, but we have gone out together quite a lot. He also stayed here over Christmas and Hogmanay and I was able to introduce him to Belinda, who was at home for part of that time.

'The lockdown has made everything very difficult and we've agreed to put things on hold until normality returns. That's especially important now that the three of you are staying here. I'll be honest that it would have been nice to have hugged Andrew when I saw him just now. But we've agreed we have to obey the rules and keep socially distanced from each other.'

'It sounds like you are giving him up so you can look after us,' said Quoia. 'That doesn't seem fair.'

'We still talk,' said Fliss. 'I was chatting to him on the phone while you were watching *The Greatest Showman* on Thursday evening. That's why I wasn't with you part of the time. I don't want you feeling guilty about a decision I took. For the most part I'm very happy with how things are working out. I've told you before that I'm less lonely with the three of you living here and that's true. Anyway, I've grown a little cautious about getting too involved with anyone since Jim died. This pause in things between Andrew and I is helpful because it gives both of us a chance to work out what we really want from life. If we still want to be together when normality returns, then we'll know for sure it's the right thing to do.'

'Did Daddy know about Andrew when he asked you to look after us?' asked Quoia.

'No, he didn't. And I'd be grateful if none of you tell him. It would make him feel guilty for asking me to take you in and I don't want that.'

At that moment Fliss's phone rang. She looked at the screen.

'It's Erica Durand. I'll go downstairs to talk to her.' Fliss headed towards the top of the stairs. 'Hello Erica, how are you?'

'Do you think we can go outside and say hello to the gardener?' asked Jude, after Fliss had descended out of sight.

'I'm not sure Fliss would think that's a good idea,' said Quoia. 'It might embarrass him. And even though we'd be sure to keep two metres distance it would probably be better not to have met him in case Mummy or Daddy ever ask. Besides, your painting is coming on really well. You don't want to leave it just now, do you?'

The children turned back to their projects.

When Fliss came back upstairs she was smiling again. 'Erica rang to say that she has to go into her office in Edinburgh this afternoon. The children are old enough for her to leave on their own at the cottage and that's what she usually does. But Jamie has asked if he can come and play in the garden here with Jude. The twins have suggested that you two, Quoia and Kaleb, might like to help take Oban for a walk again, then come back to the garden with them. It's a really nice day out there, though not as warm as on Sunday. I told her I'd ask you, but I said I thought you'd like the idea. Anyway, I said I'd text her to confirm. What do you think?'

'It's a brilliant idea,' said Jude. 'What will you do, Fliss?'

'I'll carry on with my Sandwood Bay painting. You know where I am if you need me, but you'll need to remember about social distancing and Jamie can't come in the house. Quoia and Kaleb, you will also need to remember about distancing when you're walking the dog with the twins. What do you think about the idea?'

'Yes, it's something we'd like to do,' said Quoia. She looked at Kaleb, who nodded.

'That's great. I'll text Erica. I've sanitised the racquets and the boules and left them on the patio table, with the folding chairs, also sanitised, leaning against the garage wall by the badminton net. Can we skip the swing-ball today?'

Jude nodded.

'Good. I don't really want to have to hammer it into the newly-mown back lawn. That reminds me that I need to check what time Andrew expects to finish. I'm sure it will be before Jamie comes, though. Then I'll make some lunch.'

'You can hug Andrew if you want,' said Quoia. 'I know it's against the rules, but they are saying that coronavirus doesn't really put children at risk, so we'll be OK.'

'That's a nice thought, Quoia, but I really don't think it would be a good idea. I'll go down and talk to him now.'

After Fliss had gone downstairs, Jude stood up from his easel. 'I bet she does hug him anyway. Should we see if we can see them through the big window at the back of the kitchen or from the balcony?'

'Sit down, Jude!' said Quoia. 'We can't spy on Fliss like that.'

'What about rolling up the blind on one of the back windows in here, just a little, so we can see out into the garden but it's not obvious?'

'No! That would be a horrible thing to do.'

'I was only joking,' said Jude, looking hurt.

Kaleb knew that Jude hadn't been joking. He was sure that Quoia knew it too.

CHAPTER EIGHTEEN

Florence, Isobella and Oban were waiting a little way along the track from the main road.

'Hello, I'm glad you could come,' said one of the twins. 'It's me, Isobella, by the way.'

Kaleb saw that today Isobella was in a green hooded sweatshirt with 'University of Stirling' on the front in large white letters. Florence was wearing a black zip up jacket.

'It was a good idea to meet,' said Quoia. 'You're not going to suggest we go to "The House With 46 Chimneys" again are you?'

'No,' said Isobella. 'We didn't think that either you two or Oban would be happy with that idea.'

'We thought we'd go the other way, to the Pineapple,' said Florence. 'If the gates are open again, we can sit on the grass and talk.'

'We found that a smaller gate into the garden, in the corner you get to from the forest, was locked yesterday,' said Quoia. 'That might mean the main gate was locked too, we didn't go there.'

'It's not a problem either way,' said Florence. 'So long as we can talk.'

'You've not got the same top as Isobella on under that jacket, have you Florence?' asked Kaleb. 'That would be confusing.'

Florence laughed. 'No, just a red T-shirt. We've tried that trick on you already and we know people get tired of it.'

'Before we set off,' said Quoia, 'do you promise to tell us about your family's links with the house and about the ghost story you mentioned?'

'We're both sorry about Sunday,' said Isobella. 'There just wasn't time and we had to talk about what had happened first anyway. But I guarantee we'll tell you the story today.'

'All right, thank you. I was disappointed but I do understand. If you and Oban stay to the left side of the track and Kaleb and I to this right side, then we can talk while we walk.'

No-one said anything until they'd turned left at the T-junction of tracks and had started to walk through the avenue of Redwoods.

'I'll start,' said Isobella. 'It's a complicated story and it might be easiest if I start in the middle, with the cottage.'

'The cottage you are living in?' asked Kaleb.

'Yes. I think we told you that it was given to an ancestor of ours by the family who owned the estate in 1887.'

'The Murray family, the Earls of Dunmore?' asked Quoia.

'Yes, that's right. I'll come to the interesting part, why we think they did that, in a moment. First, though, I'll tell you that the person the cottage was given to was called Mary Simmonds and she had previously worked as a lady's maid in Dunmore Park.'

'Mary's daughter was called Rose, who married a schoolteacher in Airth, Arthur Murray. He was a distant relative of the Murrays who owned the estate, but he wasn't rich. They lived in the cottage with Mary. Rose and Arthur Murray, and Mary Simmonds, all died in February 1919 of Spanish flu, which was a little like coronavirus only, it seems, far worse.

'Rose had a daughter in 1897. It was the month after Queen Victoria's diamond jubilee, so they called her Victoria. Victoria married a man called Albert Gordon in Edinburgh in 1918 when she was 20. Albert also died of flu in 1919, though by this time Victoria was expecting a child. She called the child Mary, after her great grandmother. The two of them moved to the cottage in Dunmore in 1919.'

'After her husband, her mother, her father and her grandmother had all died of flu?' asked Quoia. 'That must have been hard.'

'It must,' said Isobella. 'If we move forwards a generation, Mary Gordon got engaged to a man who joined the army and was killed at Dunkirk in 1940. She never married but did have a daughter later in 1940 who was called Lily.'

'Was Lily your grandmother?' asked Quoia.

'That's right. She married a man called Michael West in 1965. He ran a pub in Edinburgh. They had three children, the last of whom was Mum, Erica, who was born in 1975. Our grandad, Michael West, died in a car crash in 1979. Mum barely remembers him. After he died, Grandma Lily moved back to the cottage with the three children, just like Mum has done more recently. Mary lived until 2000, when she was 81. As you know, Lily lived until last year.'

'Did your grandmother tell you all this?' asked Quoia.

'She did,' said Isobella, 'but we've done a lot more research over the past year, online at Ancestry.com and in other places.'

The walls of the garden were now in sight. 'It looks like the gates are locked again,' said Kaleb. 'That's a shame. I wanted to sit on the grass in front of the Pineapple.'

'It's not a problem,' said Florence. 'That stone wall round

the car park is low enough to sit on. If we take the two sides of the corner there, we can talk easily enough without being within two metres of each other. Let me just take Oban to explore in those trees first.'

After Florence returned and sat down, Isobella started talking again.

'I said at the beginning that the important question is why Mary Simmonds was given the cottage by the Dunmore Park estate in 1887. We think we know why that was, but this is mainly down to what Grandma Lily told us.

'I said that Mary Simmonds had a daughter, Rose. Rose was one of twin sisters. The other was called Ruby. They were born in February 1873, so in April 1887 they had recently turned fourteen years old. They were employed as kitchen maids in the house. As I said, their mother, Mary, had a much more important job as a lady's maid, looking after the lady of the house. Their father, Peter Simmonds, worked as head groom in the stables.'

Out of the corner of his eye, Kaleb saw Quoia look meaningfully at him.

So did Florence. 'What is it?' she asked.

'There's something we need to tell you about the stables,' said Quoia. 'But you finish your story first.'

'All right,' said Isobella. 'We know that Ruby and Rose shared a room in the servants' quarters high in the north range of the house. Mary Simmonds lived nearer the family's rooms and Peter Simmonds had a room in the stable block.'

'On the night of the 8th of April 1887, Ruby was returning to her room from the kitchen, where she'd done the last jobs needed to shut everything down for the night. In the corridor leading to their room she saw a ghost moving towards her. She was at the top of the steps up from the kitchen and must have forgotten where she was, because she moved backwards and fell down the steps, breaking her neck and dying as a result.'

'Oh, no!' said Quoia. 'That's horrible.'

'Can I ask a question?' said Kaleb.

'Of course,' said Florence.

'If Ruby died, how do we know she saw a ghost? She'd not have been able to tell anyone.'

'We know, or think it's highly likely,' said Isobella, 'because Rose also saw the ghost. As she later told it, she came out of their room because she sensed something was wrong with Ruby. She saw the figure of a girl moving along the corridor, away from Rose but towards where Ruby was standing at the top of the stairs. The girl shouted, 'Somebody please help me!' and Ruby stepped back and fell as she passed. Other servants with rooms on the corridor came out because they heard Ruby scream as she fell, but no-one except Rose heard the ghost say anything or saw her.'

'Are they the same stairs?' asked Kaleb. 'Was Ruby at the top of the same stairs that Quoia and I and Oban felt something at the bottom of?'

'We're not certain,' said Isobella, 'but we think so.'

'That's really scary,' said Quoia.

'It gets worse,' said Florence. 'Rose wouldn't leave Ruby's body, which ended up part the way down the stairs from the attic to the upper floor, so they sent someone to get their mother, Mary. They also sent someone to the stables to get their father, Peter Simmonds. Just before they arrived there was a dreadful accident caused by a spooked horse that started kicking out and rearing up. Peter and another groom tried to calm it. The other groom heard Peter call out just before the horse's front hooves struck him on the head and killed him. What he shouted was, "Ruby, watch out!"'

The afternoon was now sunny and reasonably warm, even here under the shelter of the trees outside the walled garden. But Kaleb suddenly felt very cold and was covered in goosebumps.

'I heard it,' he said.

'You heard what?' asked Florence. 'You're shaking, what's the matter Kaleb?'

Kaleb just looked at the ground in front of his feet.

'Are you all right, Kaleb?' asked Isobella.

Quoia moved a little along the wall and put her arm around Kaleb's shoulders.

'We went to the stable block, yesterday,' she said. 'Kaleb heard a horse in distress and loud banging. Jude and Fliss heard nothing. I'd already been scared away by the atmosphere of the place.'

'Can you tell us exactly what happened, and where?' asked Florence.

With prompting and support from Quoia, Kaleb told the twins what had happened.

There was a long silence, broken by Oban barking once, and tugging in the direction of a tree that Kaleb hadn't seen him go to before.

'Should we head back to the village?' asked Isobella, who was holding Oban.

'Yes, I think we should,' said Quoia, standing up. 'Come on, Kaleb, you'll be fine once we get moving.'

'You do look very pale,' said Florence.

There was a short silence as they started walking. It was Quoia who broke it.

'Are you saying that the reason the Dunmore Park estate gave the cottage you live in to Mary Simmonds was that one of her daughters, Ruby, had been killed in the big house after seeing a ghost of a girl and that her husband had been killed shortly afterwards because a horse was spooked by something that might have been the ghost of Ruby?'

'Yes, and no,' said Isobella.

'That's not a helpful answer,' said Quoia. 'It also seems a very generous thing for them to have done. What happened was tragic, certainly, but if the landed gentry gave away property every time a servant died in service, they'd soon have no property left. That doesn't sound likely in Victorian times.'

'That's true. What I've told you is only part of the story. You only get the full picture by going back another two generations beyond Mary. The thing you should know is that for this last part, we are relying mainly on what Grandma Lily told us. There's not much information available anywhere else that we've been able to find.'

'Let's walk while you tell us the rest,' said Quoia.

'OK,' said Isobella. 'Let me take you back to the night of the 8th of April 1828. "The House With 46 Chimneys" had only been built for a few years and we can be sure it had more than 46 chimneys at that time. Amongst the servants were two fifteen-year-old housemaids. They were twins, Rose and Lily Robertson.

'That night someone killed Lily Robertson by striking her on the head with a poker. A cousin of the family, Edward Murray, was staying at Dunmore Park at the time. He was 22 but already had a reputation as a gambler and a drinker and it seems he'd been sent here by his family to keep him out of trouble. It didn't work.'

'Did he kill Lily?' asked Kaleb.

'Yes,' said Isobella. 'Down in the basement of the house there are lots of wine cellars. One of them, beneath the entrance hall, is octagonal and, in its centre, there is a small

147

room that was always locked. That was where they kept the best wines.'

'We've been in there,' said Quoia. 'Was that where Lily died?'

'No. That night, the other twin, Rose, had gone down to the basement to get some wine from one of the other wine cellars when she heard a noise in the octagonal room. When she went to check, she found Edward Murray coming out of the usually locked room carrying two bottles of wine. It later emerged he had paid a footman to allow him to use the key whenever he wanted. He'd been stealing some of the family's most expensive wine since not long after he arrived, two weeks earlier.

'Edward offered Rose money to pretend she'd seen nothing. When she refused to take it, he grabbed her and tried to strangle her, but she managed to break free and hid in one of the other cellars until he left. It seems he was so desperate to silence her that he then went to the north range and waited for her in the attic corridor, where the servants had their rooms. By chance, Lily finished her work for the night not long afterwards. She returned to the room she and Rose shared. Only she didn't get there. Edward Murray mustn't have known that Rose had a twin and hit Lily over the head with a poker in the corridor, apparently after chasing her along it. Another servant saw him waiting in the corridor before Lily arrived. They thought it was odd but only realised the significance afterwards.'

'You are saying that he killed the wrong twin?' asked Quoia.

'That's right,' said Isobella.

'What became of him?' asked Kaleb.

'Everyone in the house knew what had happened, and why,

but it was covered up. Nothing was done officially. But a month later the family sent Edward off to take up a post with the East India Company in India. He disappeared from the ship taking him there when it was off the coast of South Africa. The story Grandma Lily passed down to us is that he jumped overboard because he was full of remorse about killing the original Lily. We will never know.'

'How does this connect to what you've told us already?' asked Quoia.

'The surviving twin from the earlier pair, Rose, later had a daughter called Lily, named after her dead sister. And Lily later had a daughter called Mary who, after she was married, was known as Mary Simmonds. She, of course, was the mother of the later twins, Ruby and the other Rose.'

Kaleb had been concentrating on what Isobella had been saying. 'Does that mean that the Ruby who died in 1887 was the great-granddaughter of the sister of the Lily who was killed in 1828? That would mean that it was seeing the ghost of her great-grandmother's sister that caused her to fall down the stairs to her own death?'

'That's right,' said Isobella.

'But I'm still not clear why Mary was given the cottage,' said Quoia.

It was Florence wo replied. 'Grandma Lily told us that the Murray family gave Mary Simmonds the cottage because, like our family, they believed that the deaths of Ruby Simmonds and her father Peter Simmonds could be traced directly back to Edward Murray killing Lily Robertson. Grandma Lily told us that she thought they were trying to draw a line under an unhappy time in their history. Perhaps the idea was that by doing right by Mary Simmonds they would prevent future hauntings of their house.'

Isobella picked up where Florence left off. 'You say you've not been able to find anything about ghosts at Dunmore Park, Quoia. Neither have we and we've been looking ever since Grandma Lily told us the story. It seems their plan might have been successful, certainly for as long as they lived there.'

'But we've felt them, and I've heard them,' said Kaleb.

'That's true,' said Isobella. 'We're not sure what to make of that or why you can sense them when we can't.'

'There's another thing,' said Kaleb. 'You said that Lily was killed on the 8th of April 1828, and that Ruby died on the 8th of April 1887. It's the 8th of April tomorrow. Aren't you scared?'

'You mean because one of each of the last two sets of twins in our family has died on the 8th of April in Dunmore Park?' asked Isobella. 'Yes, as the third set of twin girls in the family we're very worried. But what can we do? Mum would simply laugh if we tried to talk to her about it. Telling you two means we have at least shared the story. But it's worse than you know. The 8th of April 1887 was a full moon. Tomorrow is also a full moon.'

'What about 1828?' asked Quoia.

'No, the 8th of April was only a half moon that year, so the pattern doesn't work. On the other hand, there was no ghost that night, just an evil man who wanted to keep a secret. Look, we're back at the main road. You lead on and we'll wait here for a few minutes then drop Oban off and come to your aunt's garden.'

CHAPTER NINETEEN

Jude and Jamie were playing badminton on the back lawn when Kaleb and Quoia returned to Forthview House. Kaleb got lemonades from the kitchen for Quoia and himself and they sat on the rattan sofa watching the boys play.

When Florence and Isobella arrived, they were carrying a cool box with some cold bottles of Coke inside. This stopped the game while they and Jamie had a drink and afterwards everyone sat on the grass, in two safely distanced family groups.

Kaleb didn't pay much attention to what the others were doing. He found himself thinking about what the twins had said instead. After a while someone started an 'I spy' game. They'd not been playing this for long before Fliss came out to say that Erica was home and she wanted the children to go back to the cottage for their tea.

Fliss cooked spaghetti bolognese and afterwards the children watched TV in the lounge while she worked on her painting in the studio. Quoia texted Mummy and Daddy separately to try to set up a Skype call with them but didn't get a reply from either. Kaleb played games on his iPad, not really paying much attention to what was on the TV.

Not long before Kaleb's normal bedtime, he heard Fliss's phone ring in the studio. He could hear she was talking to someone but nothing else over the sound from the TV. The conversation seemed to last for some time. He wondered if it was Andrew the gardener.

When Fliss walked through into the lounge Kaleb looked up from his armchair by the window. She looked really upset. Quoia and Jude were on the sofa so had their backs to her.

'Can we turn the TV off, please?' asked Fliss.

'Aw,' said Jude, 'it's just getting to the best bit.'

'No arguments. This is important.'

Quoia reached over and picked up the remote, which was by Jude, and turned the TV off.

'What is it?' she asked.

Fliss walked over to stand in front of the TV and turned to face Quoia and Jude. 'That was your mother on the phone. Henry, your dad, has had an accident and is in hospital.' She held up her hands as all three children started to speak. 'Hang on, your mother says he's going to be fine, but he's likely to be in hospital for a few days.'

'What happened?' asked Quoia.

'Apparently there was an accident on the Edinburgh city bypass earlier this evening. They think a wheel fell off a van. This caused a crash with several other vehicles, including your dad's car. He was on his way back to Kirkliston from work at the Royal Infirmary. Your mother said that if the road had been as busy as in pre-lockdown days it could have been far worse, but it sounds bad enough as it was.

'Your mother's been told that your father has got a broken arm and some cracked ribs, and he also had a bash on the head that might cause concussion, as well as some other cuts and bruises. She's seen him and talked to him. He's unhappy that his injuries will stop him working, which she took as a good sign.

'Apparently, because of coronavirus, no friends or relatives

152

of anyone in hospital can visit. She told me that when she was contacted about the accident, she went anyway. She used her warrant card to gain access. She was unofficially "investigating the cause of the accident", as she put it. Even so she had to dress up in protective gear to see him. She rang me from the hospital car park and asked me to tell you what had happened. I think she intends to go straight back to work in Livingston to see if she can find out anything more.'

'Did she sound all right?' asked Quoia.

'She sounded upset, to be honest,' said Fliss. 'I got the impression she'd tried to be very calm and official while in the hospital, but once she started talking to me it all caught up with her.'

'Is there anything we can do?' asked Jude.

'I asked whether any of us could help in any way. She said we were helping simply by keeping each other safe here. It meant she didn't have to worry about you at a time when she was worrying about your father. I said I would talk to Granny and Grandad Dalgleish in Melrose. It's been a very long time since I've talked to either of them, but I owe it to Henry, and to them, to let them know what's happened and to tell them that your dad will be all right.'

'Haven't you talked to them since the lockdown began?' asked Jude.

Fliss laughed, bitterly. 'I think the last time I spoke to them was to tell them that Jim had died. The last time I saw them was at his funeral.'

'You didn't speak to them at his funeral?' asked Kaleb, surprised.

'No, they came to the cremation. I saw them sitting near the back. They didn't come to the gathering for our friends afterwards. Henry and Anna came to both, though come to think of it, that's probably the last time I saw your mother. My parents saw Belinda and David sometimes when they were children, but again not often.'

'Why?' asked Quoia.

'Why do I have so little to do with them? It's a long story that goes a long way back. We disagreed about most things when I was a girl. We especially disagreed about the subjects I should do at school and what I should study at university. I wanted to study art and your grandparents wanted me to study medicine. They had to wait another ten years before they could persuade Henry to study medicine instead. We had no contact for years after that, not until David and Belinda came along.'

'That's really sad,' said Quoia. 'With lots of people dying now of coronavirus, especially old people, I think you should try to build bridges with Granny and Grandad.'

'I agree,' said Jude, to Kaleb's surprise. 'They are both really nice people and you are a really nice person. You shouldn't allow what happened long before any of us were born make things worse than they are already.'

Kaleb could tell that Fliss was also surprised by Jude.

'What about you, Kaleb?' she asked. 'Should I tell my parents that all three of their Dalgleish grandchildren think their grandparents and aunt are being stupid for letting the past get in the way of things now?'

'Yes,' said Kaleb. 'Please also tell them that we're thinking of them and hope we can see them again soon.'

Kaleb could see tears forming in Fliss's eyes.

'OK, I will,' said Fliss. 'Look, it's your bedtime, is there anything you want before we go downstairs for your story? I think it's my turn to read tonight.'

After Fliss had finished two chapters of his book and gone

upstairs, Kaleb put his glasses back on. Tonight, he didn't want to look out of his window. Instead he picked up his phone and sent a short text to his father, telling him to get well soon. He didn't know when Daddy would see it or be able to reply, but it felt better to have sent it. Then he sent a text to Mummy saying he hoped she was all right and telling her that he loved her.

A few minutes later he got one back from Mummy, thanking him and telling him that she loved him too. And telling him that he should be asleep by now.

*

In his dream, Kaleb saw a big chestnut brown horse with a white blaze on its face, rearing up above him and whinnying. Then something broke into the dream and pulled him from one world back into another. He lay on his back, wondering what had woken him.

After a second, he heard the front doorbell ring. There had been enough deliveries to the house over the past week for him to know its tone well. Then someone banged on the door four times.

Kaleb put his glasses on and walked out into the corridor. This always had a light on at night, like the hall. As he passed Jude's bedroom door his brother appeared, looking sleepy. They stopped at the end of the corridor and Kaleb peered round the corner, towards the front door. This had a narrow glass panel in the centre, but though he could see the security light outside was on, Kaleb couldn't see anything else. On the opposite side of the hall he could see Quoia peering round the edge of her bedroom door, looking scared.

There was more banging, then a man's voice called, 'Come

on Fliss, I know you're in there. You've been blanking me. I need to talk to you.'

Then Kaleb heard something else, a more distant woman's voice.

The man continued, a little more quietly but still loud enough to hear clearly in the hall. 'There you are, Fliss. I need to talk to you.'

'I think he's gone,' said Quoia, after a moment.

'We need to make sure Fliss is all right,' said Jude. 'I think he went towards the drive, which is where Fliss would have appeared. Let's see if we can see anything from your bedroom window, Kaleb. Yours is the nearest to the drive.'

The three children hurried along the corridor and into Kaleb's room, where he cautiously rolled up the blind a little.

'Make sure the door's closed so no light shows through from the hall,' said Quoia to Jude.

'I can't see anything,' said Kaleb. I can't even see if there's another car on the drive, though you can tell the security light on the front of the garage is on, like the one by the front door.'

'You're right, the angle doesn't work,' said Quoia. 'Look, let's try to open your window just a little. Enough to allow us to hear what's happening outside.'

In the darkness, Kaleb saw Quoia cautiously lift the handle and push the window. It opened a little, making almost no noise.

'Shush!' said Quoia, quietly.

'Look, John,' said Fliss, from out of sight to the left. 'I've already told you twice. I can't help you. I'm sorry, truly I am. But I just can't.'

'Can't or won't?'

'You've known since the beginning of the year what's happening. I simply can't help you.'

'You'll regret this, Fliss. I'll be back and I won't be alone.'

'Don't be stupid, John. Just get in your car and go away. And don't come back, ever.'

'I'm serious, Fliss. You can't do this.'

'Well I have done it. And there's something you ought to know. I'm in the garage apartment because I've got my niece and two nephews staying with me. I'm sure you'll have woken them up by banging on the door. Their mother, my sister-in-law, is a detective inspector with Police Scotland. What's the betting that they are calling her right now, telling her someone's trying to break into my house?'

'You'd never dare involve the police.'

'It's not me who's involving them,' said Fliss.

Kaleb heard the man swear at Fliss. Then he heard a car door slam shut and a light-coloured car reversed out onto the lane from the drive and then sped away towards the village.

There was a pause.

'Are you all right, children?' said Fliss as she appeared right next to the window, making Kaleb jump. 'Yes, I saw the window open and guessed I'd find you in there. My friend John didn't see it, thankfully.'

'Yes, we are, Fliss,' said Quoia. 'Are you?'

'I'm a bit shaken, to be honest. 'Let's meet up in the kitchen in a few minutes for a cup of cocoa and an explanation. And in case you've been wondering, I only said that bit about you calling your mother so I could get rid of our visitor, not because I want you to do it.'

*

They sat and drank their cocoa in silence.

Then Fliss spoke. 'I said I'd give you an explanation. I'm

sorry that happened. It was the last thing I wanted. Look, if I promise to tell you absolutely everything, will you let me hold off giving you that explanation until Thursday?'

'Why?' asked Quoia.

'I'm just asking the three of you to trust me. Look, it's Tuesday night.' Fliss twisted round to look at the clock on the kitchen wall. 'Actually, it's very nearly Wednesday morning and we could all do with getting back to bed. I do promise that I'll be completely open with you on Thursday.'

Kaleb saw Quoia look at him, and then at Jude.

'Fair enough,' she said. 'But the explanation's got to include why you went to deliver a painting to someone in Stirling yet didn't actually take a painting out to your car.'

'It will.'

'And why you took two bags of paints to a friend in Greenock but left one of them in your car.'

'Ah, I wondered if you'd seen that. That was careless of me. Yes, I promise to explain that too. For my part can I ask the three of you not to tell your mother about any of this. Not until you've heard my explanation anyway.'

'Hang on,' said Jude.

'Fliss is right,' said Quoia. 'Let's remember that Mummy will be really worried about Daddy. The last thing she needs is any reason to worry about us, too.'

'I agree,' said Kaleb.

'What about you, Jude?' asked Fliss. 'This is only going to work if all three of you agree to keep this a secret until Thursday.'

'OK,' said Jude. Kaleb could see how reluctant his brother was but thought that having given his agreement he would stick to it.

'That's good,' said Fliss. 'If everyone's finished their

cocoa, then it's time to get back to bed.'

CHAPTER TWENTY

WEDNESDAY THE 8TH OF APRIL 2020

Kaleb realised that the scene he found in the kitchen as he got to the top of the stairs was one that he was getting used to seeing each morning. Jude and Quoia were eating cornflakes. Fliss was drinking coffee. Perhaps she'd finished her toast, he thought, though he couldn't smell any.

'Ah, you're up!' said Fliss. 'I've just said to Quoia and Jude how sorry I am for the disturbance last night.'

'I know you said you'll explain everything tomorrow, Fliss,' said Quoia, 'but…'

'I will, I promise.'

'Yes, but you can at least tell us who that man was. He was threatening you. What if he comes back today?'

'He won't, I'm sure of it,' said Fliss. 'But I really don't want you getting anxious about him. If it helps, his name is John MacDonald and he lives with his wife and two children in Bridge of Allan, north of Stirling. I think her name is Jessica, but I've never met her. I know him because I used to teach him, quite a long time ago. Can everything else wait until tomorrow? Please?'

Quoia said nothing, Kaleb watched as she looked away from Fliss and caught his eye. He could tell she was regretting agreeing to wait for an explanation until Thursday. He knew, though, that Quoia would feel bound by what she had agreed to. He had the feeling that Fliss knew it too.

The silence that followed was awkward.

'Right,' said Fliss, 'we need to talk about today's schoolwork.'

'Oh, no,' said Jude. 'We had a disturbed night and lost a lot of sleep.'

'I think the last part of that might be a slight exaggeration, Jude,' said Fliss, smiling. 'But it's shaping up to be a lovely day outside, so I thought we'd go on a history field trip.'

'Where to?' asked Jude. 'I'm sure Stirling Castle is closed because of the virus, like everywhere else. Anyway, we went there with Daddy last year.'

'Fliss, have you heard anything from Mummy about Daddy?' asked Quoia.

'No, I'm sorry. I'm sure she'll let you know as soon as she hears anything. Perhaps the three of you should agree a text message to send to her to cheer her up and remind her you are thinking of her and of Daddy? If you send her a single message with all your names on, then she knows that she only has to reply to that when she does have something to tell you.'

'That's a good idea,' said Quoia.

It didn't take them long to write a short message on Quoia's phone, which she then sent to Mummy.

'You were talking about a history field trip,' said Jude.

'Yes, I was,' said Fliss. 'It will mean a ten-mile drive there and the same back.'

'That's against the rules, isn't it?' asked Jude. 'Just like when we went to see the broch and the castle.'

'That's true,' said Fliss. 'It needs to be something we've all agreed to. If we were stopped, I suspect my claiming it was an educational trip might not be seen as "essential travel". I'd be responsible and I am happy to take that risk, but I don't want to involve you three unless you want to go.'

'Where would we be going?' asked Jude.

'To the remains of a Roman fort called Rough Castle, which is on the line of the Antonine Wall. That was a wall the Romans built across the narrowest part of Scotland.'

'A bit like Hadrian's Wall?' asked Quoia.

'Well it wasn't built of stone, so there's less remaining, but the idea was the same.'

'And it's a choice between going ten miles to see these castle remains or staying here and working?' asked Jude.

*

The traffic was light. Just before they turned off the motorway, Quoia received a text on her phone.

'Mummy says she's going to see Daddy this morning,' she said. 'She's heard he's all right, well, apart from the obvious injuries we already know about. She'll text again after she's seen him. She's not supposed to visit, but being in the police helps.'

As they drove into Bonnybridge, Fliss asked, 'Who knows what a U.F.O. is?'

'It's an unidentified flying object,' said Kaleb. 'Spaceships and aliens and all that. I don't think they exist outside of films and TV programmes.'

'And books, of course,' said Fliss. 'There are some people who think they are real, but they are very much in the minority. I have read that Bonnybridge, this place, is called the U.F.O. capital of Scotland because of the number that are said to be seen here.'

'That's all rubbish, isn't it?' asked Jude, looking a little concerned.

'Very probably, Jude. They're certainly nothing to worry

about. Right, if I remember correctly, this minor road turns into a track that leads to the car park. I have to admit that I last visited when we were still living in Stirling.'

'There's a gate blocking the way,' said Quoia.

'Yes, that's to be expected given the lockdown. I think there was a closed gate on my last visit too, possibly because it was winter. We can park this side of it without causing an obstruction, while keeping our distance from this car.'

'Does the car mean there will be other people visiting?' said Jude.

'Yes, but not many. We'll keep away from them if we see them.'

After they'd parked and hats, boots and sunscreen had been checked, Fliss led the way through a metal pedestrian gate that she carefully opened with a piece of kitchen roll in her hand.

'Right, come on through and I'll close the gate.'

'Is that the Antonine Wall?' asked Kaleb, pointing at a broad, deep ditch that ran away from them across the ground. As it neared the skyline it was possible to see there was a mound running along the side of the ditch nearest them.

'That's right,' said Fliss. 'Tell me then, who knows anything about the Romans in Scotland?'

'Not much,' said Quoia. 'I know they did come to Scotland, and I had heard of the Antonine Wall, but I'd not have been able to tell you what it was or where it was.'

'Well that's something at least,' said Fliss. 'Many people believe that the Roman Empire stopped at Hadrian's Wall and it was only blue-painted savages to the north of it.' She looked at the boys. 'How about you two?'

'Sorry, no,' said Jude.

'I think I saw a documentary Daddy was watching on TV that talked about it,' said Kaleb. 'But I was playing on my iPad so didn't really take much notice. It showed some Roman baths at a place near Glasgow.'

'That would have been Bearsden,' said Fliss. 'Look, it's not far along the line of the wall to get to the remains of Rough Castle. I'll give you a little background while we're walking.'

Kaleb listened while Fliss talked.

'The Romans invaded what's now Scotland three times. From AD 80 to 84 they seem to have got a long way north before defeating the Caledonians at a huge battle called Mons Graupius. That was probably in Aberdeenshire. That invasion was led by their governor of Britain, Julius Agricola. Before he could complete his conquest of Scotland, he was recalled to Rome and his successors were happy to build a defensive line of forts some way north of here and regard that as the edge of the empire.

'In AD 105, they withdrew to the line on which they later built Hadrian's Wall. In AD 139 they invaded again, occupying Scotland as far as a line between the River Forth and the River Clyde. Three years later they started building the Antonine Wall, which took two years to complete.

'In AD 170 the Romans again abandoned Scotland and withdrew to Hadrian's Wall. Then, in AD 208 the Roman Emperor Septimius Severus launched the Romans' final campaign to try to conquer Scotland. He died in AD 211 with the job only partly done. The following year his successor as emperor abandoned everything north of Hadrian's Wall for the third and final time.'

'Wow,' said Jude. 'That's confusing. So, they spent two years building this wall and then abandoned it after less than thirty years?'

'That's right Jude,' said Fliss, smiling.

'What a waste.'

'What would it have looked like, Fliss?' asked Kaleb.

'You have to imagine that the wall itself was on the south or right-hand side of the ditch as we're seeing it. They'd have laid stone foundations over four metres wide with a turf wall built up on top of that to a height of maybe a little less than four metres. There was probably a wooden walkway on top, with a wooden barrier on the north side of the walkway to protect the soldiers.

'Then, in front of the wall, on the northern side, was the ditch. This would have made the wall seem much higher to anyone approaching from that side. Behind the wall, on the south side, was a road called the Military Way that allowed rapid troop movement along its length. The wall was 37 miles long and approximately every two miles the Romans built a fort to house the troops manning the wall.'

'Is that the fort there, on the far side of the valley ahead of us?' asked Kaleb.

'It is,' said Fliss. We need to descend to the wooden bridge across the stream in the valley, then climb up the other side to the fort.'

In Kaleb's mind, there was only one thing wrong with the view ahead of them.

'It's a shame that they've got those two lines of pylons and power cables running right across the line of the wall,' said Quoia, echoing his thoughts. 'It really destroys the atmosphere.'

'That's true,' said Fliss. 'Look, from here you can see, despite the cables, that the fort was built in a classic Roman playing card shape. They've excavated the fort in the past and found it once had several large stone buildings within the outer ramparts. Let's go and look. Let these people cross the bridge first.'

Fliss and the children stood back while a middle-aged couple crossed the burn in the other direction, smiling a greeting as they passed.

The children spent some time amongst the series of humps and bumps that was all that was left of the fort.

Fliss had wandered off a little to one side. When she rejoined them, they had some water and biscuits.

'Who has heard of Camelot?' she asked.

They all had.

'How would you feel if I told you that you were standing in Camelot now?'

'Cool!' said Jude.

'That's amazing,' said Kaleb. 'But are we really? I thought King Arthur was based in Cornwall.'

'I thought it was in Wales,' said Quoia.

Fliss laughed. 'I think you can take your pick. But I did read a book once that said that in the 500s, what was left of the Roman fort here was used as a war base by a prince called Artuir. He was the oldest son of a king of Dalriada, the kingdom that held this part of what later became Scotland. The book claimed that this was the start of the legend of King Arthur and Camelot. I don't know if it's connected, but there's a place called Camelon only a mile or so towards Falkirk from here.'

'But it could be lots of other places, too, couldn't it?' asked Quoia.

'Yes, it could. But it's a bit like the U.F.O. stories back in Bonnybridge. You make your own mind up what you believe or not.'

'Are we going back, now?' asked Jude.

'There's one more thing I want you to see first,' said Fliss. 'By far the coolest thing here.'

'What is it?' asked Jude.

'I want the three of you to go over in that direction, beyond the line of the ditch, and tell me what you find. You'll need to be careful where you put your feet, though.'

Jude ran off, with Kaleb a little way behind. He saw Jude stop and caught him up. In front of them was an area completely covered by lines of holes in the ground. Each hole had curved ends and was perhaps two or three times as big from end to end as it was from the near side to the far side.

'What are these, Fliss?' asked Jude as Fliss and Quoia joined them.

'They are called *lilia*,' said Fliss. 'The Roman soldiers dug pits. Then they placed sharpened stakes in the pits, with the pointed ends upwards, and tried to conceal them with brush or vegetation. Anyone attacking the fort from this northern side would be in for a very unpleasant surprise. If nothing else, it would have broken up any attacks. Right let's head back to the car.'

As they crossed the bridge over the burn, Kaleb saw Quoia look at her phone.

'I've had a text from Mummy,' she said. 'Daddy's going to be in hospital for a few days yet. They've got to do an operation on his arm to make sure he keeps the full use of it. She says it's not something to worry about. Otherwise he's better than he was last night. She says we can talk to her on Skype this evening.'

'That's something to look forward to,' said Fliss.

Just before they got to the pedestrian gate that let them through to where they'd left the car, Quoia touched Kaleb's arm. They were behind Fliss and Jude. She put a finger to her lips in a 'shush' gesture and passed Kaleb her phone.

She'd had a text from Florence. Kaleb read it. *'Isobella and*

I need to talk to you and Kaleb. It's really important and it has to be today. Any ideas?'

Kaleb handed Quoia's phone back to her. She raised her eyebrows at him for a moment then put her phone back in her pocket.

CHAPTER TWENTY-ONE

Fliss, with help from Jude, made sandwiches for lunch.

'What are we going to do this afternoon, Fliss?' asked Jude. 'It's too nice to stay in.'

'You're right,' said Fliss. 'For early April we've been having an amazing spell of weather. It's like the weather gods know we're all locked down and are playing a joke on us.'

'At least we've been out,' said Jude.

'That's true,' said Fliss. 'But you have to remember that the four of us have broken the lockdown rules several times now. We should have stayed here, and only gone out for exercise to places we could walk to from the house. We also broke the rules by having the Durand children come to play in the garden and by having Erica visit. Even going out and walking the dog with them was against the rules.'

'But we kept a safe distance all the time,' said Jude.

'I know we did,' said Fliss, 'but you have to remember that's not the point.'

'Are you saying we can't do that anymore?' asked Jude.

'No, I just want all of you to keep in mind that we've been doing things we shouldn't talk to anyone about. Your father wasn't happy when he found out we'd been to the broch and the castle. Your mother won't be happy if she hears we went even further away to visit the Roman wall and fort. Or if you tell her anything about the Durand children.'

'I understand, Fliss,' said Jude. 'I'm sure we all do.'

'The other thing to keep in mind is how lucky we are,' said Fliss. 'Imagine if you lived in the centre of a city, perhaps in a flat, and couldn't get out. Imagine how people with small children manage in circumstances like that. Think what it would be like being stuck in all the time with noisy neighbours in the flats either side of you and above you. Think about the homeless people you used to see begging whenever you were in the centre of Edinburgh. I've no idea how they are coping with the lockdown.'

'That's all true,' said Quoia. 'We do know how lucky we are to be here with you, Fliss, and we're really grateful.'

Fliss smiled. 'Sorry, I wasn't looking for gratitude, it's just that I really worry how some people cope. I also worry how any of us will cope when this thing comes to an end. It's going to have left such a deep mark on everyone, even those of us in comfortable surroundings.'

'When do you think it will end, Fliss?' asked Kaleb.

'I just don't know. I don't think anyone knows.'

'And in the meantime, people can't visit their relatives before they die or even go to their funerals afterwards,' said Quoia, with tears in her eyes.

'Look, I'm sorry, Quoia,' said Fliss. 'I didn't mean to upset you. I just sometimes feel the whole thing is getting on top of me. It's wrong to make you unhappy by talking about it.'

'I think it helps to talk about it, Fliss. We all think these things. It doesn't help to keep it inside and pretend that nothing is wrong.'

'I suppose you're right,' said Fliss. 'Look, I'm not sure how the conversation took that turn, but we do need to answer Jude's question about what we're going to do this afternoon. Any ideas?'

'Can we see Florence, Isobella and Jamie again?' asked Quoia.

'I'll call Erica and ask what their plans are for the afternoon. Not that many people really have plans during the lockdown.'

'Perhaps, this time, Jude and Jamie could take Oban for his walk while the rest of us sit in the garden.' said Quoia.

'That's not fair!' said Jude and Kaleb, together.

Fliss laughed. 'I think that's your answer, Quoia. It looks like the same arrangement as yesterday, if that's all right with them.' Fliss picked up her phone and walked to the top of the stairs. 'Right, I'll call Erica. Can Kaleb and Quoia do the washing up as Jude helped make lunch?'

*

The twins identified who was who when Quoia and Kaleb met them in the usual place on the track beyond the main road. Kaleb thought Oban seemed especially pleased to see him but knew better than to ask to hold the dog's lead.

Little was said until they got to the entrance to the walled garden.

'The gates are locked again,' said Quoia. 'Should we sit on the wall like we did yesterday?'

After they'd sat down, the twins seemed more interested in the ground in front of them than in their surroundings. Oban nuzzled Florence's leg, as if trying to get her attention. After a moment she leaned down to stroke his head.

'Your text said it was really important and we had to meet today,' said Quoia. 'What's wrong?'

We want to ask you something,' said Florence. 'We don't think you are going to like it.'

171

'What is it?' asked Quoia.

'We have to go to the ruined house tonight, late tonight, after it's properly dark. We want you two to come with us. Not Jude and not Jamie and certainly not Oban, just the four of us.'

'No way!' said Quoia. 'That place creeps me out in the sunshine. I'd never go anywhere near it in the dark.'

'We thought you'd say that, Quoia,' said Isobella. 'We can't make you come with us, but you have to realise this may be the only chance we will ever get to find out more about what happened all those years ago.'

'Why?' said Quoia.

'This may be complete nonsense,' said Isobella. 'But Ruby saw the ghost of Lily on the 8th of April and she fell down the stairs to her death as a result. It was a full moon that night. Today is the 8th of April and tonight the moon will be full. If we are ever going to see Lily's ghost, then tonight is our best chance.

'Before you say anything, I know that the two of you, and Oban, have experienced things in the right part of the house on other days and when the moon wasn't full, and in daylight. But Florence and I haven't, even though we've been there. We desperately want the chance to see or feel something for ourselves. We believe we must try tonight. There might not be another full moon on the 8th of April for years and years to come.'

'Don't you think it's dangerous?' asked Kaleb. 'We talked yesterday about what happened to Ruby and to Lily. They were each part of a pair of twins and they were both members of your family, and they both died on the 8th of April in Dunmore Park. You two are twins, the third set in your family. Isn't it asking for trouble for you to go anywhere near the old house on this date given what's happened twice before? And if

172

the full moon does make a difference, then doesn't that make it even more dangerous?'

Florence looked up. 'We talked about that a lot last night. We know you're right but we both think we have no choice. What happened back in 1828, and then in 1887, has hung over the women in our family like a cloud for generation after generation. We might have somewhere to live as a result of it, a cottage that those women have retreated to time and again when their lives have gone wrong, but that's not much of a consolation.'

'What I don't understand is what you think you'll achieve by going to the house tonight,' said Quoia. 'What if you did see Lily's ghost? Or Ruby's for that matter? How would it help?'

'We don't know. We just believe we have to go,' said Florence, looking miserable. 'We don't want to go, believe me. Well I don't certainly. But the thought of looking back in a year's time, or five years' time, and knowing we did nothing when we could have tried to do something is unbearable.'

'What I don't understand is how it might work once you are there,' said Kaleb. Everything above the bottom few stone steps has gone in that part of the north range. The corridor in the attic where Lily was killed, and where her ghost caused Ruby to fall, just isn't there anymore.'

'Again,' said Isobella, 'we don't know. You are right. At most there might be some vertical walls at that level of the building, but even that's only true for the bit of the north range that wasn't demolished. But you two, and Oban, felt something down in the basement, so who knows?'

'Why do you want us there?' asked Quoia.

Kaleb though he knew the answer to that question. He thought that Quoia already knew it, too.

'You've both sensed things there,' said Isobella. 'We haven't. We need you there because we think you might be able to help us. At least you can tell us if you feel something or not.'

'Oban could tell you if he felt something or not,' said Quoia. 'You don't need us.'

Then she smiled and Isobella and Florence laughed. It took Kaleb a moment to see what was funny.

'No, I suppose you'd just say that was being cruel to Oban because he's no way of understanding what's happening,' said Quoia.

'Will you come with us, then?' asked Isobella.

Kaleb could feel that Quoia was looked at him and turned to meet her gaze.

After a moment Quoia said, 'We will.'

Kaleb had a sinking feeling in the pit of his stomach.

CHAPTER TWENTY-TWO

Kaleb thought that the rest of the afternoon and evening passed painfully slowly. Fliss had made a nice tea. Then they'd had a Skype call with their mother who seemed reasonably cheerful, if very tired. The operation on their father's arm had gone well and now he just needed time to recover.

They knew that Fliss usually went to the apartment above the garage not long after Quoia and Jude were in bed and tonight it had been the same.

The time between Kaleb going to bed and 9.50 p.m. just didn't seem to want to pass. He'd set an alarm on his phone but, although he had slept a little, he was awake before it went off.

Then he got dressed and very quietly went to meet Quoia in the utility room, where they put their coats and boots on. The weather forecast said it was going to be a reasonably clear night but quite cold.

Kaleb had agreed with Quoia that if they went out of the front door it would set the security light off and could wake Jude, whose bedroom was nearest the door. They therefore went out of the utility room door into the garden and through the gate at the back corner of that side of the house. Quoia had tried it earlier to make sure it didn't squeak.

The small gate from the front garden into the lane did groan a little, which caused Kaleb's heart to skip a beat, but not so much that he thought that Jude would hear.

It was a huge relief to be clear of the house. The village was deserted and there was no traffic on the main road. The moon, which was full and seemed enormous, was now visible off to the left, not yet very high in an almost clear sky. Florence had told him earlier that it was due to rise a little before 9 p.m.

There was enough light from the moon to see the track and the two dark shapes standing beside it a little ahead of them.

'You came,' said one of the twins. 'Thank you. We weren't sure if you would.'

'Well we did promise,' said Quoia. 'How do we tell which of you is which in the dark?'

The speaker laughed. 'We thought of that. I'm Florence and I'm wearing a woollen bobble hat and a thick stripy jumper. Isobella has on a dark jacket. With so much light from the moon, that should be enough to allow you to tell who's who.'

'Did you bring torches?' said Isobella.

'Yes,' said Quoia, 'and we found some spare batteries without Fliss knowing. Look, should we go? I'm getting cold standing here.'

Kaleb was pleased when they moved off, keeping on the opposite side of the track to Florence and Isobella to maintain social distancing. Kaleb realised that this had become a habit.

After they turned off the track, the path through the woods seemed extremely dark and more than a little scary.

'I think we're going to have to use our torches,' said Quoia.

Florence led.

'Are you sure this is the right way?' asked Isobella, not long after the same thought had begun to prey on Kaleb's mind.

'Yes, you get occasional glimpses of the moon through the trees, so we're certainly going in the right direction, though we may not be exactly on the track.

'Are there any animals in these woods?' asked Quoia, again not long after the same thought had occurred to Kaleb.

'I suppose there are deer, I don't know,' said Florence. 'Why?'

'I thought I heard something behind us,' said Quoia. 'It was making the same sort of noise we're making as we walk.'

'I heard it too,' said Kaleb.

'Let's stand still and see if we hear anything,' said Florence. 'Can you shine your torches in the direction you heard the noise? We'll then do the same. If there is a deer or a fox or a badger or something, then we might see the reflection of the torchlight from its eyes.'

The children stood where they were. Kaleb couldn't see anything in the light from their torches. The noises he'd been hearing had stopped.

'No, nothing,' said Quoia.

'Well let's go on then,' said Florence. 'Distances seem much longer in the dark but I'm sure we're almost there.'

Florence was right. Not far beyond where she'd been standing, she came to a halt again. Kaleb saw her flicking her torch around and realised she was close to where they'd first stood and looked at the ruin of Dunmore Park with Fliss.

As he and Quoia joined the twins, Kaleb again thought he heard a noise from the woods behind them. He shone his torch back that way and had the impression of something moving, but it was so fleeting that he might have imagined it. He felt the hairs in the back of his neck and his arms rising, even under his clothes.

'We need to decide what to do about the torches,' said

Isobella. 'We had no choice in the woods, but there's enough moonlight to see without them here. And if we use the torches it will harm our night vision and make us more dependent on them.'

'I agree with you about the moonlight,' said Quoia. 'But if you look down into the basement level of the ruins, there are large patches of really dark shadow everywhere. It would only take one of us to stand awkwardly on a bit of stone to break an ankle. That really would be a bad end to the night.'

'OK,' said Isobella. 'We'll use the torches when we have to. Kaleb, you found the steps last time we were here. Can you lead and we'll be close behind you?'

'Two metres behind?' asked Kaleb.

'Well yes, if you want,' said Isobella, 'but without sensing anything special, I'm finding this a really scary place right now. How would you feel about holding my hand, with Florence and Quoia just behind us holding hands too?'

'Why?' asked Quoia.

'We don't have to,' said Isobella. 'But it would mean that the two of you who have felt something here would be holding hands with the two of us who haven't. It might help increases our chances of sensing what's here. And it might give you a little reassurance when you do feel something.'

'What about social distancing?'

'As you said this afternoon, what happened to Lily and Ruby in this house makes this feel an extremely dangerous place for Florence and me right now. Somehow social distancing seems much less important when balanced against that.'

'If Kaleb's happy with that, then so am I,' said Quoia.

Kaleb reached out and took Isobella's hand and the two of them walked carefully down the ramp that led down to the basement level. They were quickly in shadow and had to use their torches with their free hands to watch where they were putting their feet. He could hear Quoia and Florence just behind them and see the flicker of their torches.

'It's just round here,' he said. 'Through this doorway and on the left. Here we are.'

'What do you feel?' said Isobella.

'I'm scared, to be honest. But I don't really feel anything else. Not like I did the last two times I came here. Last time the feeling got stronger and stronger, so I can't be sure. What about you, Quoia?'

'I sense something but it's nothing like as strong as it was last time. It makes me uneasy standing here and looking at those steps in the torchlight, but I can still stand here. Last time I didn't get this close in daylight before I needed to run away.'

'Should we wait for a little while to see if you feel any more?' asked Isobella. 'I don't feel anything beyond disappointment and frustration.'

'I'm the same,' said Florence. 'Last time you had goosebumps, Kaleb? Have you got them now?'

'Well I have, but I got them when we were standing outside because I was sure I saw something move in the trees behind us. They've not gone away, but they've not got worse.'

Isobella let go of Kaleb's hand.

'I'm going to climb up these steps,' she said. 'They look solid enough.'

'Be careful, said Quoia.

Kaleb watched as Isobella climbed up one step and then another. At the top she followed the turn round, so she was facing back out towards the other three.

'That's as far as it goes,' she said. 'I was sort of hoping that something might happen. I hoped climbing the steps might trigger something that the two of you could feel.'

'Sorry,' said Quoia.

'I don't know,' said Kaleb. 'When you're concentrating on it you can't really tell whether it's changing. I do think I feel something now, but it's not getting any stronger and its far weaker than it was last time.'

'Well I suppose that's it,' said Florence. 'At least we tried.'

Kaleb could hear the disappointment in her voice. Isobella had edged her way back round the turn at the top of the steps and was climbing down the last few to the floor of the alcove.

'What's that?' she said, pointing her torch over the heads of the other three.

'What did you see?' asked Florence.

'I'm sure I saw someone through a gap over there.' Isobella pointed. 'Only for a moment, and when I shone my torch there was nothing there.'

'Was it a person?' asked Kaleb. 'Or could it have been an animal?'

'I don't know. It's a bit spooky though, isn't it? Especially after you saw something outside, Kaleb.'

'Look,' said Florence. 'We're in a creepy old ruin that's got a ghost story associated with it and two of you have been genuinely frightened here before. It's no surprise if we start to see things that aren't there, because we're looking for them and expecting to see them. Hoping to see them, even.'

'I suppose you're right,' said Isobella.

'I think we should call it a day, or a night,' said Florence. 'We said we'd regret it if we didn't come here and try to find out more about what happened. Well we've tried. We've got the right date and it's a full moon, just like it was when Ruby saw Lily's ghost. I think we've done everything we possibly can. I think we should go home now. I'm just grateful to Quoia and Kaleb for coming and trying to help, even though you didn't want to.'

'Yes, thank you,' said Isobella, who was now back on the floor of the alcove.

'You're welcome,' said Quoia. 'But we've not yet done everything we possibly can, have we?'

'What do you mean?' asked Isobella.

'Now we've come this far, I think we should go to the stables,' said Quoia. 'If you go home now, sooner or later you'll start to wonder if you missed your chance to find out what you want to know. If we go to the stables and find there's nothing there, then you really will know you've done all you can.'

Kaleb couldn't quite believe the change in Quoia. He'd have thought the last place she'd want to go just now was the stable block.

It was Isobella who replied. 'But both Lily and Ruby died somewhere above us in this part of the house. And it was up there that Ruby saw Lily's ghost.'

'Quoia might be right,' said Florence. 'It's not far and it would stop us wondering if we missed something. We should go.'

With that, the four of them picked their way back to the ramp.

Florence led the way round the outside of the north and west ranges and past the grand entrance to the house, then along the broad track towards the stable block.

The moonlight illuminated the side of the block but left the front totally in dark shadow. As they passed the castle-like corner where Kaleb had heard the horse, he felt the onset of what was now a familiar feeling. At the same time, Quoia stopped walking.

'Are you all right, Quoia?' asked Florence.

'I'm getting the same feeling I had last time we were here,' said Quoia.

'Me too,' said Kaleb.

'Oh, wow!' said Florence. 'It looks like it was worth coming here. Let's hold hands again. I'll hold yours, Quoia.'

Kaleb felt real fear as he passed between the half-open gates and into the passageway beyond. Holding Isobella's hand helped him and kept him moving forwards. Again, they had their torches in their free hands. The far end of the passage and the near part of the courtyard was in what now seemed bright moonlight. But with the moon low in the sky, much of the courtyard was in the dark shadow cast by the building. As before, the trees in the courtyard made it impossible to see very much at all, only it was worse in the dark.

'The place you were talking about is off to the left, isn't it?' asked Isobella.

Kaleb nodded, then realised she'd probably not be able to see him. 'Yes, it is.' His throat felt very dry. 'It's an old yellow door in the corner, standing open.'

Isobella looked behind them. 'How are you doing, Quoia?'

'My legs feel like jelly and I want to run away but holding Florence's hand helps.'

Isobella moved slightly ahead of Kaleb, but still held his hand, as they made their way along the short path to the corner of the courtyard.

'Was it this door here?'

'Yes, that's the one,' said Kaleb, who now felt as if all the hair on his head was standing on end.

They moved through into the hallway beyond the door. Florence and Quoia followed. Kaleb turned and touched

Quoia's arm. He saw her smile at him in a flicker of torchlight, but he could feel her arm was shaking badly.

'Is this how it was when you were last here?' asked Isobella.

'Yes,' said Kaleb. 'Fliss and Jude came in with me. Jude went over to the bottom of those steps over there and shouted out something like "Is anybody here?".'

'And that was when you heard the horse?'

'Yes, that's right.'

'Does anyone feel like shouting?' asked Isobella.

'I really don't think that would be a good idea,' said Quoia.

'Hang on,' said Kaleb. 'Can anyone smell anything?'

'I've just got a really strong stable smell,' said Isobella.

'Me too,' said Florence. 'But surely the stables here have been disused for decades?'

'I can smell the same thing,' said Quoia. 'I think it's coming from behind this wooden door.'

She pointed at the door on the right-hand side of the hallway.

'That's where I heard the horse, last time,' said Kaleb.

'There's a doorknob,' said Isobella. 'Who wants to turn it?'

There was complete silence in the hallway. Kaleb felt utterly terrified. He could see from the look on Quoia's face that she felt the same.

'I will,' said Florence.

Kaleb saw Florence turn the knob and push open the door, which creaked loudly. Then she went through, pulling Quoia, whose hand she was still holding, behind her. Isobella followed, giving Kaleb no choice but to go with her. The door closed itself behind him, leaving the four of them in total darkness as their torches had all gone out. Kaleb felt intensely cold for a moment, then the feeling passed.

'What's happened?' said Quoia.

'Hang on,' said Florence. There was a bright light. 'That's it. I had to turn my torch off and back on to get it to work.

'Mine's the same,' said Quoia.

Four beams of light darted around the space they stood in.

'It's stables,' said Isobella. 'There must be a dozen stalls along here on the left, with wooden fronts. And there's straw on the floor.'

A noise caused Kaleb to shine his torch into the stall nearest the door, the one he was standing next to.

'There's a white horse in this one.'

'No wonder it smells of stables,' said Florence. 'There are horses in the next two stalls as well. I think there might be horses in all of them.'

'But this is weird,' said Quoia. 'You said this place had been disused for decades.'

'Or longer,' said Florence. 'But there's no getting away from the fact that we are looking at horses now. I mean, it can't be a mass hallucination can it?'

'I don't know,' said Isobella, 'but I can't imagine that hallucinations smell this strongly.'

Quoia had taken her phone out of her pocket and looked at it. 'Can everyone check their phones?'

'What are we checking for?' asked Isobella.

'Mine's dead, as if the battery's flat. I've tried turning it on from scratch. That worked with the torch. Is anyone else's working?'

No-one's was.

'What can have caused that?' asked Florence.

'I don't know,' said Quoia 'But I'm beginning to have a suspicion.'

She walked over to the door they'd entered by and tried to

turn the doorknob. 'It won't move. It's like it's completely solid.'

'What's your suspicion, Quoia?' asked Florence.

'That maybe we're not in 2020. Everything just feels totally different.'

Isobella laughed. 'Well that would be a neat way of beating coronavirus, wouldn't it? Simply go somewhere that it isn't.'

'You're serious, aren't you?' asked Kaleb.

'Yes, I am,' said Quoia.

There was a long silence in the stable.

Then Florence laughed, nervously. 'There's something I've always wanted to be able to say, ever since we saw *The Wizard of Oz* when we were little.'

'What's that?' asked Quoia.

Florence laughed again, still nervously. 'Toto, I've a feeling we're not in Kansas anymore.'

CHAPTER TWENTY-THREE

'So now what do we do?' asked Kaleb.

'We don't seem to have a lot of choice,' said Quoia. 'This door won't move. Let's try the bigger one at the far end.'

'Hang on,' said Florence, letting go of Quoia's hand. She walked to the door they had entered by and pulled on the doorknob. 'You're right. It won't even rattle. It's like it's not a door.' She pulled at the knob again, then shrugged and walked back to the others, who were now standing a little way along the stables.

'Is it me, or are the horses starting to move around more?' asked Kaleb, whispering.

'You're right,' said Isobella. 'Look, let's keep as quiet as we can. We don't want them getting disturbed and making lots of noise.'

At this point a horse further along the row of stalls whinnied.

'We need to get out of here,' said Isobella, walking towards the far end of the stables.

As Kaleb followed, he looked at where the whinny had come from and saw a large chestnut brown horse with a white blaze on its face looking back at him from the stall next to the end of the row.

'I saw that horse in a dream last night,' he said. 'I also think it's the one I heard last time I was here.'

'It's looking right at us,' said Quoia, 'as if it's interested in what we're doing.'

Isobella suddenly stopped. Kaleb, distracted by the horse, walked into the back of her. He realised that the large door they were now only a few metres from had opened towards them. Two men in old fashioned clothes and carrying oil lamps walked in.

'Well I can't see what the problem is,' said one of them. 'Can you have a quick look at them all, Charlie, starting at the far end? I'll see if Sultan's all right. I think it was him I heard.'

'I'll do that, Peter.'

Kaleb followed Isobella as she jumped to one side to let Charlie past. The man paid no attention to the four children, even though he walked right by them. He went to the far end and slowly walked back along the line of stalls, lifting his oil lamp so he could see each of the horses in turn.

Meanwhile the other man, Peter, was saying something Kaleb couldn't hear to the big chestnut horse, Sultan, and running his hand gently down its face.

'They all seem fine to me,' said Charlie.

'I think Sultan just wanted some attention,' said Peter. 'He's had it now. That ought to keep him happy for a while.'

Charlie was the first to leave. Before he closed the door behind him, Peter stood still for a moment and took another look round the stables, his gaze appearing to pass right through the children.

When the door closed, Kaleb felt the breath he'd been holding for what seemed like forever burst out of him.

'That was weird,' said Quoia. 'They just didn't see us at all.'

'Our torches are still switched on,' said Florence. 'They didn't see us or the light from them.'

'I'm not so sure,' said Isobella. 'When that man Charlie walked towards me, I thought he was going to collide with me. I jumped to the side and just for a split second I thought he'd sensed something. But then the moment passed, and he kept on walking. It might just have been a trick of the light. It was a bit of an odd effect having both oil lights and torches.'

'We really do need to get out of here,' said Quoia. 'Before the horses start making too much noise again. Sultan certainly seems to know we are here. The door the men came through is obviously the one they use to get the horses in and out by.'

Quoia had reached the door by now and pulled on the handle. 'I didn't hear them lock it, but it's solid, like the one at the other end.'

'Let me try.'

Kaleb saw Florence reach past Quoia for the handle before both girls gasped.

'My arm went straight through the door!' said Florence.

'I know, I saw,' said Quoia, reaching out for the handle again. 'It's solid to me. You try Kaleb.'

To Kaleb the door handle seemed quite immovable. Then Isobella tried. He saw her arm disappear up to the elbow. She snatched it back, then cautiously tried again, with the same result. Then she reached over and touched the wall on one side of the door before walking over to the first of the stalls in the stable and touching the wood that formed its front.

Isobella looked at the others. 'Everything else seems solid and real. It's just the door that's not.'

Florence repeated her sister's actions. 'Likewise. But for me, the door at the other end, the one we came in by, was also solid.'

'I didn't have a go at that one,' said Isobella. 'Let me try something, though.'

With that she put an arm in front of her face and walked at the door, then disappeared into it. She was back a moment later.

'I can pass through the door!' she said with a look of shock on her face. 'On the other side there's an open fronted passage that leads out into the courtyard. I couldn't see much because it's dark.'

'That's fine for the two of you,' said Quoia, 'but Kaleb and I are stuck here with these horses. We can't open either door.'

'Give me your hand, Kaleb,' said Isobella. 'Right, put your other arm in front of your face so you don't bang it on the door. That's it, now follow me!'

Kaleb saw Isobella pass into the door, as she had a few moments earlier. Then he felt something like the shock he'd once got by touching the electric wire round a farmer's field with a piece of grass. Then he was standing in a dark passage with Isobella. She pulled him away from the door just as Florence and then Quoia came through it, holding hands.

'Well that's closed doors sorted,' said Isobella, looking pleased with herself in the torchlight.

'How did you know holding hands with you two would get Kaleb and I through?' asked Quoia.

'Honestly? I didn't. But I couldn't think of anything else and it seemed worth a try. What do you think we should do now?'

'I suppose that depends why we're here,' said Quoia. 'It also depends when this is.'

'What do you mean?' asked Florence.

'Look in the courtyard,' said Quoia. 'The far side is brightly lit by moonlight, like when we arrived. Only now the little we can see looks well cared for and there are no trees. We can't see from here, but what's the betting that when we get over there, we'll see it's a full moon?'

'Are you thinking this is the 8th of April 1887?' asked Isobella. 'I can't get my head round that. But then I can't get my head round walking through a closed door, and we've all just done that.'

'You talked about Ruby's father being killed at the stables on the same night that she died,' said Kaleb. 'Wasn't his name Peter?'

'Yes, Peter Simmonds, the head groom,' said Florence. 'Could that have been him, do you think? Could we have just met our great, great, however many times great grandfather?'

'Wouldn't that be amazing?' said Isobella.

'In my dream, Sultan was rearing up and whinnying,' said Kaleb. 'Sultan was also the horse that seemed to react to us most. I think it was Sultan that killed Peter Simmonds.'

'But perhaps not "was",' said Quoia. 'If Peter is still alive then that's not happened yet. I think Sultan is going to kill Peter. And if it's a full moon tonight then it could well be the right date, which would mean that the two deaths are going to happen tonight.'

'Do we have any idea when?' asked Florence.

'If you think through the story,' said Isobella, 'the only part that might allow us to attach a time is that Ruby went up to the attic corridor after she'd done the last jobs needed to shut everything down for the night. The problem is that we have no idea when that would happen in a house like Dunmore Park in 1887. I don't know if it makes any difference that it was a Friday night. Would the family have been entertaining? Would that have kept the kitchen open later? We just don't know.

'All we really know is that what happened to Peter here in the stables seems to have quickly followed what happened to Ruby at the top of the stairs up to the attic corridor. We also believe that what happened to Peter was directly caused by what happened to Ruby.'

'I agree,' said Florence. 'If we're to understand what really happened that night, we need to go to the house itself.'

'That sounds like asking for trouble to me,' said Quoia, 'But I suppose it's only the same as my thought earlier, that you can't give up looking now, when it seems you're so close.'

'That's decided, then,' said Isobella.

Kaleb followed Isobella across the courtyard. When they got into the moonlight on the far side, she looked back over her shoulder and he did the same. It was a full moon, just as it had been when they had arrived at the stables. Only, it seemed, it was now 133 years earlier.

CHAPTER TWENTY-FOUR

The large doors to the stable block were wide open and what they could see of the area in front of the stables in the shadow of the building looked beautifully manicured. Kaleb realised Isobella had stopped when he again walked into her. She'd switched off her torch and he did the same.

'Look at that!' she said, pointing towards the ruined house.

Only, Kaleb realised as he looked, it wasn't a ruined house. In the moonlight it looked simply magnificent.

'Oh, wow!' said Florence. 'That's what "The House With 46 Chimneys" looks like when someone cares for it and it has more than 46 chimneys.'

'You can understand just how badly it's been swamped by modern trees when you see it without them,' said Quoia. 'And what we know as fields are now gardens. Look on the right, in front of the south range. There's a stone ha-ha there that you'd never know had ever existed when you see the area in 2020.'

'What's a ha-ha?' asked Kaleb.

'That stone wall you can see, with lower ground to the right of it as we're looking. It separates the garden immediately in front of the house from the land beyond it without putting a barrier in the view.'

'You can see lights in a few of the windows,' said Kaleb. 'Not bright, like modern lights, but you can still see them.'

'I suppose they used oil lamps back then,' said Quoia. 'Like the ones Peter and Charlie were carrying. Or candles. Have you noticed? It's much less cold now than it was earlier. We seem to have gone back to a milder night.'

'I still can't believe this isn't a dream,' said Florence. 'Can someone pinch me?' She yelped. 'I didn't mean that literally, Isobella!'

'There's a carriage in the main entrance,' said Kaleb, 'There are people getting into it.'

'I think that's where we have to go next,' said Isobella. 'This drive looks very grand when it's not just the bit that's left between two farmer's fields.'

As they neared the house the carriage, pulled by two dark-coloured horses, pulled away from the entrance and headed towards the children.

'We need to hide!' said Florence.

'No, just stand still until it passes us,' said Isobella.

The drive was wide enough to mean the carriage passed some metres away from them. Nonetheless, Kaleb found it hard to stand still when it felt like they were so exposed in the moonlight. He couldn't see who was in the carriage but the figure of the coachman was very clear.

It was worse when they got to the entrance.

'There must be other ways in, at the back,' said Florence. 'You can see through the window in the door that there's a footman in a coat and top hat just inside the hallway. If we open the front door he's bound to notice.'

'Who said anything about opening it?' asked Isobella. 'We'll just go through it.'

'What do you think, Quoia?' asked Florence.

'There's another carriage coming,' said Quoia. 'You can hear it. Let's give it a go while we can.'

Kaleb thought it would have been far better to go round to

the back of the house and try to find a way in there. But he'd not been asked for his opinion and didn't think this was the moment to be difficult.

Isobella took his hand again and walked under the carriage entrance, which was lit by oil lamps either side of the front door. Then she led him through the door without opening it. Kaleb felt the same shock as before, though this time he was expecting it, so it wasn't as bad. Florence and Quoia followed.

The octagonal entrance hall was beautifully decorated. It was difficult to believe it was the same place as the hollow, ruined shell he'd seen when they came with Fliss.

The footman was holding open the door from the room at this end of the south range. An elderly couple who looked like aristocrats in a period film walked through into the hall.

The man pulled a watch out of a breast pocket and looked at it. 'Our carriage is late.'

Kaleb wished he could see what the watch said, then realised there was a grandfather clock standing against one of the angled walls of the room. It said that the time was nearly 11.30 p.m.

'We're last away as usual, Charles,' said the woman. 'I wish that just one night you'd realise that you will never be as good a backgammon player as the Murrays. How much did you lose tonight?'

'Not much. Not much.'

Isobella pulled Kaleb's hand and he followed her through, again literally, a door leading into the west range of the house. The corridor beyond was in darkness. Florence and Quoia didn't follow for a few minutes and when they emerged on the other side, they looked shaken in the light of Kaleb's torch.

'That was close,' said Quoia. 'It was fine when the two of you went through the door, but when we started to move it

194

was if the woman could see something or sense something. She pointed straight at me and said she'd seen something move out of the corner of her eye. We'd stopped by then and she decided it was nothing. When nobody was looking at us, we moved again.'

'I suppose it's all part of learning how we fit into this really odd 1887 world we've found ourselves in,' said Isobella. 'We obviously need to be careful because we aren't totally invisible to everyone here, especially when we move. But whatever we've got still seems better than Harry Potter's invisibility cloak.'

'We don't know if they can hear us or not,' said Florence.

'That's true,' said Isobella. 'We need to be careful about that.'

'Now we're here, where should we go?' asked Kaleb.

'I think we have to find a way of getting to the attic corridor in the north range,' said Isobella. 'That's where Ruby saw Lily's ghost and fell to her death. I'm worried that we may not have much time. Did anyone else notice the time on the clock in the entrance hall? It's really late and while we don't know how the house works, it has to be shutting down now the last guests have gone.'

The ground floor of the west range was dark and deserted and the children found their way with their torches.

'I think we've now turned into the north range,' said Quoia. 'As we're on the ground floor, the attic corridor ought to be two floors above us.'

'There are steps here,' said Isobella.

'Should we follow them up to the top of the house?' asked Quoia.

'They're not THE steps,' said Isobella. 'They're at the wrong end of the north range. But they would be the quickest way up to the corridor.'

She turned towards them and lifted her leg as if to start the climb. But then she recoiled back and ended up sitting on the floor.

'What happened?' asked Florence.

'Ow, that hurt!' said Isobella. 'It was like there was a solid wall I couldn't see, blocking access to the stairs.'

Quoia walked to the bottom of the stairs and reached out a hand, wiggling her fingers. 'There is something solid here.' Then she moved her right foot, as if to place it on the bottom step, then stopped. 'You're right. We can't use these steps.'

'But they're the quickest way. Kaleb give me your hand. Let's try together.'

Kaleb gave Isobella his hand.

'No, that's no good either,' she said after being repelled again.

To Kaleb it had felt like a solid wall was preventing them starting the climb up the stairs.

'Let's carry on along the ground floor of this range until we get to more stairs,' said Isobella. 'We know there are some at the far end, even if there are no others.'

She and Kaleb bounced off the next door they tried to walk through. Isobella hit her head quite hard, though Kaleb had been protected because she'd been in front of him.

'That hurt even worse,' she said. 'I'm not sure what we do now. The door's just solid and immovable and stops us going any further along the north range.'

'Why don't we see if we can go down the stairs back there?' asked Kaleb. 'We only know we can't go up them. Then we might be able to go along at the basement level to the bottom of the other stairs, the ones we've seen in 2020.'

'It doesn't seem likely, does it?' said Florence.

'It's worth a try though,' said Quoia.

While the stairs leading upwards remained blocked, the children had no problem descending to the basement of the north range. This was also dark and deserted.

A little further on, Quoia stopped by an open door leading off the corridor they were in. 'That looks like the kitchen in there.'

They went in.

'It's huge,' said Florence.

'More importantly, it's dark and empty,' said Isobella. 'That means Ruby has already gone upstairs.'

They went back out into the corridor.

'Brr!' said Quoia, 'Does anyone else suddenly feel cold? Since we left the stables, I've been feeling overdressed, but now I'm shivering.'

The others could all feel it too.

'Here are the steps,' said Isobella. 'They must be the ones I climbed earlier. We need to get up to the attic corridor as quickly as we can. Are you all right, Quoia?'

'No, sorry. I couldn't feel anything here earlier, but right now it's the strongest I've ever felt. It's like a horrible cold black fog of fear and its wafting down from higher up the stairs.'

'What about you, Kaleb?' asked Isobella, shining her torch on him. 'Good grief, I can see you shaking. Hold our hands and we'll help you get up the stairs.'

'I'm sorry,' said Quoia. 'It's as much as I can do to stand here. I just want to run away. I simply can't go up those stairs.'

'Can you Kaleb?'

'Sorry, Isobella, no.'

'I understand, but we have to go. Wait for us in the kitchen.'

With that, Isobella took Florence's hand and the two twins bounded up the stairs.

'We shouldn't have let them go on their own,' said Quoia.

'We couldn't have stopped them,' said Kaleb.

'But one of each of the last two sets of twins in their family has died on those stairs, or at the top of them. I just know something dreadful is going to happen.'

A loud scream from somewhere above suddenly echoed down the stairs.

Then there was a second scream, slightly less loud.

'Oh, no,' said Quoia. 'I knew it.'

There were more noises from further up the stairs that sounded like a girl wailing.

'It's all right,' said Kaleb. 'Well, it's obviously not all right, but I think I heard Rose calling out Ruby's name. That might mean Florence and Isobella are safe.'

CHAPTER TWENTY-FIVE

The minutes that followed seemed to Kaleb to be the longest of his life. He found himself listening intently to the noises coming from higher in the building.

'We ought to go and find Isobella and Florence,' said Quoia.

'Are you able to go up the stairs?' asked Kaleb. 'I don't feel any happier about this place now than I did when the twins asked us to go with them. But I'll come with you if you really want to go.'

'No, you're right,' said Quoia. 'Most of me wants to go back to the kitchen and away from these horrible steps. If we did that it would seem like we were betraying them.'

She paused for a moment. 'Did you feel that? It was like a sudden wave of extreme cold coming down the stairs and sweeping past us. Now it's much less cold.'

Kaleb had felt exactly what Quoia described.

'Yes, I did,' he said. 'The crying and wailing from upstairs stopped at the same time.'

Kaleb held Quoia's hand as they stood and waited.

'Listen!' Quoia said. 'Now there are footsteps coming down from the floor above.'

Kaleb and Quoia switched off their torches and moved to one side of the alcove, away from the bottom of the steps.

There was a loud whisper. 'Quoia? Kaleb? Are you there?'

At the same time Kaleb saw the flicker of torches coming down the steps. He thought that if it was 1887 then there were probably only two people in the whole world other than Quoia and himself who had electric torches. He switched his own on and Quoia did the same.

'We're so glad to see you,' said Florence, who was first down the last few steps.

'Are you all right?' asked Quoia. 'You look like you're crying.'

'Look, let's go to the kitchen and talk there,' said Isobella, who pushed past Florence and led the way.

The others followed. The kitchen door was closed, which Kaleb thought was odd. He remembered it being open.

Isobella took his hand and they passed through. She stopped immediately on the other side and Kaleb walked into her as he emerged from the door. He in turn was bumped into by Florence.

'Give us some room!' said Florence.

'Shush! Look!' whispered Isobella.

Kaleb had moved to one side so he could see the kitchen properly. What had been dark and empty a short time before now had a large fire at one end and four oil lamps and there was a smell of cooking. It was also uncomfortably warm. There were two girls in the kitchen and an older woman. They seemed to be busy preparing a meal.

'Back out into the corridor,' whispered Isobella as she turned and pushed him.

Florence and Quoia passed through the door ahead of him and Kaleb quickly followed.

'We must have taken a wrong turning,' said Quoia. 'That was a different kitchen.'

'I'm sure we didn't' said Isobella. 'But I agree it was

200

different. It wasn't just that there were those people there. The layout seemed different too, though I didn't have long to look.'

'We can't stand here in this corridor,' said Florence. 'Not now there are people about. Someone might come. We need to find somewhere to talk.'

'Let's go this way,' said Isobella.

She led the way along the corridor, away from the stone steps that led up to the attic. The next door on the right, the other side of the corridor from the kitchen, was closed.

'Wait here,' said Isobella. She then disappeared through the door.

She was back a moment later. 'It's some sort of store for copper pots and pans and jelly moulds. We can talk in there.'

Isobella took Kaleb's hand and led him through the door. He shone his torch around at what looked like it could be part of a museum.

'Do the two of you feel anything bad in here?' asked Isobella.

'No, for me we left the sense of dread behind as soon as we moved away from the bottom of the steps,' said Quoia.

'I'm fine here,' said Kaleb. 'How are you both though? You look really upset. What happened?'

Florence took a deep breath and spoke. 'We'd climbed up past the ground floor and first floor when we heard a girl shout out, above us, "Somebody please help me!" That must have been Lily's ghost in the attic corridor. The worst thing was that it sounded just like Isobella's voice. Then we heard a truly awful scream on the stairs just above us, which would have been Ruby falling, then we heard Rose scream and call out Ruby's name.'

Isobella said, 'We stopped just below the last turn in the stairs and turned our torches off. The noise was coming from somewhere that seemed just a few steps above us, just out of sight. Part of me wanted to go on, but most of me was horrified by the absolute awfulness of the moment. I knew that Ruby's body, and Rose, were just a short distance away, hidden by the turn. It was like I was paralysed.'

'I don't think either of us wanted to see Ruby's body on the stairs,' said Florence. 'For me that would make it just too real. Then I heard footsteps coming up the stairs from below and a young maid appeared, carrying an oil lamp. I thought perhaps she'd heard the noise and was going to see what had happened. We were trapped on the stairs and though I tried to push myself against the wall she went right through me, as if I wasn't there.'

'She passed through me too,' said Isobella. 'Just after that it suddenly got very cold for a moment and then everything went deathly quiet. We waited for a short time then put our torches back on and climbed slowly round the last turn in the stairs. There was no one there. Then we went up to the attic corridor. That was deserted too. After that we came back down.'

'I'm sorry,' said Quoia. 'It must have been horrible for you.'

'I think the worst thing was that we were just a moment too late,' said Isobella.

'Too late for what?' asked Quoia.

'Too late to find a way of doing something, to find a way of stopping Ruby falling to her death.'

'Hang on,' said Quoia. 'Is that what we're here for? I thought we were here to find out more about what happened. Trying to actually change what happened is something else again.'

'Well no,' said Florence. 'We didn't come here to change things. But when we were that close it was just so frustrating. I mean, what if we could have saved Ruby from falling? If we'd done that, we'd have stopped Peter being killed by Sultan, too.'

Kaleb could see that Quoia had her eyes closed.

'You've both really got to think about this,' she said. 'I agree. If you'd have somehow stopped Ruby falling down the stairs, then you would probably have saved her father too. But what then?'

'What do you mean?' asked Florence.

'If Ruby and her father hadn't died that night then, at the very least, the Dunmore Park estate would have had no reason to give Mary Simmonds the cottage that your family has lived in ever since. You'd be homeless.'

'Hang on,' said Kaleb. 'If you didn't live in the village then you'd never have met us, and we'd never have come here tonight. And that would have meant you wouldn't have been able to travel back in time to save Ruby and her father. So, if you had saved them it would make it impossible for you to save them.'

'That paradox isn't the worst thing about it,' said Quoia.

'What is?' asked Isobella.

'Have you heard of the butterfly effect?' asked Quoia.

'No, what is it?'

'The idea came from a story written in the middle of the 20th Century. I read it last year in a collection of the greatest science fiction stories. It's about a man who goes back in time and accidentally kills a butterfly. When he comes back to the present, he finds a huge amount is different. That one butterfly's death had effects that got bigger and bigger through time.'

'And you think that would have happened if we'd saved Ruby?' asked Isobella.

'Well, yes. We've already said Peter probably wouldn't have died and Mary wouldn't have been given the cottage. But you've also got to ask yourself how things might have been different for Rose if Ruby had lived. Might Rose have done different things and met different people? Might she have met and married someone other than the man she married, who became your many times great grandfather? Might she and this other husband have had a boy instead of the daughter she had, Victoria was it? Even if they'd had a girl, she would have been an entirely different person. Your whole family tree might have developed in a totally different way.'

'You're saying that if Ruby hadn't died then Florence and I, and Jamie, and perhaps our mother, and Grandma Lily, might never have lived at all?'

'Yes, I am.'

'That takes a lot of thinking about,' said Isobella. 'But we are alive, and I don't see how that could be undone.'

'Neither can I,' said Quoia. 'I only mentioned it because it seemed the effects might be huge.'

'I suppose it doesn't really matter either way, does it?' asked Florence. 'We didn't get there in time to save Ruby so nothing will have changed in our world.'

'That was because that first set of stairs was blocked,' said Isobella. 'It's almost as if someone didn't want us to save Ruby, so stopped us getting up to the attic corridor in time. Now that's a truly creepy idea.'

'You make it sound like we're characters in a computer game,' said Kaleb. 'We're allowed to do some things, like walk through doors or be invisible, but we're not allowed to do others, like going up that first set of stairs, because that would spoil the game.'

'What a horrible thought!' said Florence.

'We need to decide what to do now,' said Isobella. 'If Kaleb's game designer lets us, anyway.'

Kaleb was glad to see Isobella smile in the torchlight.

'What I really want to do is go home, to Forthview House, in 2020,' said Quoia. 'But we can't do that because we're in the wrong time. I think we must go back to the stables and see if we can find a way back to where we belong. That was the place where we were shifted to the wrong time so it might be the best place to look for a way of returning to the right one.'

'But we'll probably find that Peter Simmonds has been killed when we get to the stables,' said Florence. 'It must have happened by now. I imagine there will be lots of people around, which isn't going to make it any easier for us.'

'I don't think we've got a lot of choice,' said Isobella. 'Look, at a practical level, I think I saw a door that looked like it might lead to the outside when we were walking through the basement of this range earlier. I don't think it's far from here. If we can get out of the back of the house, we can walk round it and then go to the stables.'

'All right,' said Quoia. 'You should lead the way as it was you who noticed the door.'

Isobella had been right. A little further on, a short side corridor led off to their right, towards the outside of the house rather than towards the courtyard. It ended in a solid-looking door securely bolted and with a large keyhole.

Kaleb saw Isobella look at it closely in the light from her torch, then wave her hand towards it. The hand went right through.

'That's a relief,' she said. 'That's not a door I'd like to walk into while trying to get through. Come on, Kaleb, give me your hand.'

She led Kaleb through the door. They found themselves in

a sunken brick-lined area with metal steps leading up to railings and a gate above. To Kaleb, the sky seemed much less dark than earlier, but he decided that was simply because he'd come out from the even darker house.

'I think that's the way out,' said Florence, after she'd appeared, holding Quoia's hand.

They climbed the steps and passed through the metal gate, which Kaleb found an even odder experience than passing through a solid door. Beyond the gate was what seemed to be a service area with some low buildings behind the house.

'I think those are the buildings whose foundations you trip over in the woods in our time,' said Quoia. 'There are trees beyond them, but they just aren't anything like as close to the house.'

'I'm sure you're right,' said Isobella. 'What's odd is that we can see them so clearly. Everything seems lighter than it did earlier.'

'Perhaps the moon's got higher in the sky and that's giving fewer and shorter shadows?' said Quoia. 'The thing is that if you look up you can see it's less clear than earlier. There's enough light to actually see some clouds.'

'It's also got colder again,' said Kaleb. 'It's more like it was when we were walking around the ruined house when we first arrived.'

It was more a deep gloom than a proper darkness and the children didn't need their torches to see their way as they walked out from between the buildings on the north side of the house. They then walked across the broad lawn on its west side towards the drive that would take them back to the stables.

'There are still lights in the entrance,' said Isobella. 'Look, there's a carriage arriving, and someone's just come out of the house and opened the carriage door. Talk about late arrivals!'

The children stood still and watched as three people, a man and two women, got out of the carriage and went into the front entrance of the house. The children were standing on the lawn only perhaps 50 metres away, but no-one noticed them. After the carriage pulled away, they continued walking across the lawn.

At that moment, a cloud that had been obscuring the moon cleared away, leaving it visible in the night sky ahead of them.

The children all stopped walking.

'Is anyone else seeing what I'm seeing?' asked Isobella.

'It's a half moon not a full moon,' said Quoia.

'It was a half moon on the 8th of April 1828,' said Florence. 'The night that Lily Robertson was killed.'

'That's why everything suddenly went quiet in the attic corridor,' said Isobella. 'We've moved in time again, or we've been moved again.'

'It must have happened when we all felt really cold,' said Kaleb. 'We all noticed it at about the same time though you were upstairs, and we were in the basement. That's why the kitchen was different. It wasn't an 1887 kitchen anymore. It was an 1828 kitchen.'

'And it's earlier in the day,' said Isobella. 'The sun's gone down but it's not properly dark yet. That's why we can see much more. And why people are still arriving at the house. And why they were still cooking in the kitchen.'

'But why are we here?' asked Quoia. 'And whatever the reason for us being here, this is going to make it much more difficult to find our way back to where we need to be.'

'I think I know why,' said Isobella.

'I do too,' said Florence. 'It's to give us another chance to put things right.'

CHAPTER TWENTY-SIX

'What do you mean, "put things right"?' asked Quoia.

'I know what you mean,' said Kaleb. 'You couldn't save Ruby Simmonds so you're going to try to save Lily Robertson.'

It was still light enough, even without the torches, for Kaleb to see the twins look at one another in a way that seemed to have real meaning.

'That's right,' said Isobella.

'But what about the butterfly effect?' asked Quoia. 'If you save Lily now, then you also save Ruby and Peter in 59 years' time. And then all those other things might change. The ownership of the cottage would be different, and you two and Jamie might never have been born.'

'We know all that,' said Florence.

'But it could be even worse,' said Quoia. 'The changes you'd be making would start three generations earlier. Perhaps if you save Lily then, as a result, things change so much that Mary Simmonds never lives, which means that Ruby and Rose don't live either. You'd not be saving Ruby; you'd be preventing her living.'

There was a long pause. Again, Kaleb had the sense that Florence and Isobella were sharing each other's thoughts.

'We both understand what you're saying, Quoia,' said Florence. 'We can't argue with your logic. But who's to say the universe really works like that? The four of us have seen things that defy logic and science tonight. I think that we have to put common sense on one side and do what we feel we've been brought here to do.'

'Florence is right,' said her sister. 'Kaleb talked before about the way it seems we're being allowed to do some things and not others, as if we're characters in a computer game being pushed in a particular direction. We understand about the butterfly effect, Quoia. But you also asked why we're here. I think we're here so we can put right a wrong that was done in 1828, a wrong that had consequences in 1887 and has had consequences ever since.'

Kaleb saw several different expressions flit across Quoia's face in the deepening gloom.

'OK,' she said. She looked at Kaleb, questioningly. 'We've come this far with you. We'll not stop trying to help you now.'

'Thank you,' said Isobella. 'We know the way back to the attic corridor in the north range where Lily was killed by, or is going to be killed by, Edward Murray. We'd better retrace our steps.'

'Yes, and we should hurry,' said Florence. 'It would be simply too awful to be late a second time.'

'Do we need to go back to the corridor?' asked Kaleb.

'What do you mean?' asked Quoia.

'When Edward Murray killed Lily up there, it wasn't the start of what happened that night. The start was a little earlier. It was when Rose saw him with the stolen wine. Isn't that where it might be easiest to change things?'

'You're right, Kaleb!' exclaimed Isobella. 'Let's find a way down to the wine cellars. We want the octagonal one right underneath the entrance hall. There must be steps down from the west range that we walked through earlier. I didn't see any, but we weren't looking for them.'

The children walked towards the main entrance of Dunmore Park.

'There's another carriage coming,' said Florence, 'We need to be quick.'

'It's no good,' said Isobella. 'Look through the window in the front door. You can see there are people in the entrance hall. If some of them can sense us when we move, we're never going to get through the hall without being discovered.'

'Perhaps we should go round to the door we came out by, at the back of the north range,' said Quoia. 'Then we can make our way through the basement level of the house to where we want to be.'

Isobella led the way, walking quickly. It was darker now, so they used their torches more, especially when descending the metal steps to the sunken area outside the door.

'Let's hope we're allowed back in,' said Isobella, reaching out to test the door. Her hand went through.

'We knew that already,' said Florence.

'Yes, but there's no guarantee that it would work a second time,' said Isobella. 'Give me your hand, Kaleb.'

A moment later, the four of them were back in the side corridor.

'Let's go, then,' said Quoia. 'I think we turn right onto the main corridor and then left at the end to find our way through the west range.'

'That's right,' said Florence. 'Hang on, someone's coming.'

They switched off their torches, even though their light seemed invisible to the house's residents. A man carrying an oil lamp who looked like a servant passed along the main corridor, heading towards the kitchen and the stone steps.

Isobella again led the way. Once they reached the west

range, they turned into a corridor that seemed to run the length of the basement level.

'This corridor is still here in 2020,' said Kaleb. 'We walked along it with Fliss, though it's open to the sky now. At the end it brings us to where we want to be.'

'That's right,' said Isobella. 'This corridor meets the one that runs the length of the south range. When we get to that junction we turn right, and the entrance to the octagonal wine cellar is ahead of us. The small locked room is in the centre of that.'

Isobella was in the lead when they reached the junction. She looked cautiously round the corner, along the length of the corridor beneath the south range.

'There's someone at the far end. I can see an oil lamp. No, they've gone now, off into a room on the left or perhaps into the east range.'

'What should we do?' asked Florence.

'I suppose we have to wait,' said Isobella.

'This corridor under the south range is quite wide,' said Quoia. 'If we stand together in the corner there, we will be able to see what's happening in this corridor and the one under the west range while also keeping out of the way of anyone who comes along.'

Kaleb watched as Isobella pushed her hand against the door to the octagonal cellar, and then the doors to several other cellar rooms off to one side or the other of the corridor.

'They're all blocked to us,' she said. 'I hadn't thought of that possibility. You're right, Quoia. We've got no option but to wait and see what happens.'

'Should we turn our torches off?' asked Kaleb.

'Well we don't think the people we meet here, not in 1887 anyway, can see the light from them,' said Isobella. 'But I suppose it's best not to take any chances. We don't want to scare Edward Murray or Rose Robertson away.'

'Actually,' said Quoia, 'if we were able to scare either of them away before they met, that would be exactly what we need to do.'

'You're right,' said Florence. 'We don't know who to expect to arrive first. Let's turn the torches off for the moment and see what happens.'

Without the light from their torches, the basement of Dunmore Park seemed pitch black to Kaleb. The four children huddled together in the corner and he could hear the others breathing around him.

'This is seriously spooky, isn't it?' said one of the twins, Kaleb wasn't sure which.

'Yes, but it's us that don't belong here,' said Quoia. 'We're the ghosts.'

Time seemed to pass very slowly.

'What if we've got it wrong?' asked a twin. 'What if Rose and Edward have already had their encounter here and he's already in the attic corridor, waiting for her and about to kill Lily by mistake?'

'If we move now, we risk missing them here,' said the other, who Kaleb thought was Isobella. There was something slightly different about the tone of her voice. 'We have to believe we're in the right place.'

More time passed, to Kaleb it seemed even more slowly.

'Someone's coming,' whispered Quoia.

Kaleb could see an oil lamp moving towards them along the corridor beneath the south range of the house. As it got closer, he saw it was being carried by a man wearing a dark coat over a gold waistcoat that reflected the light from his lamp. He had a large black tie at his neck. His hair was dark and quite long, and he had prominent sideburns.

'That must be Edward Murray,' whispered Quoia.

'What should we do?' asked Florence.

'I said we're the ghosts,' said Quoia. 'And we know that if we scare him away before Rose arrives, we'll have done what we need to do. Let's haunt him!'

With that she switched on her torch, jumped out into the corridor in front of Edward Murray and screamed at him.

Kaleb though he saw a brief reaction on the man's face in the light from the lamp, but it quickly passed. Edward Murray simply walked straight through Quoia, leaving her looking shocked.

'Come on!' said Isobella. 'Let's all try.'

Kaleb joined in the shouting and soon the man was surrounded by the children, jumping, shouting and screaming and shining their torches in his face and around them.

It made no difference. Edward Murray just walked up to the locked door at the end of the corridor, looked round as if to check if anyone was about, and opened it with a key he'd taken from a pocket. He entered the octagonal cellar and Kaleb could see him unlock the second door, the one to the inner, more secure, room.

'Ow,' said Isobella. 'Something's stopping me following him into the octagonal cellar. Quick, you three try. We have to do something.'

None of the children were able to pass through the invisible barrier that was blocking the way past the open door and into the cellar.

'Now what do we do?' asked Isobella.

'There's someone coming along the corridor beneath the west range,' said Florence. 'It must be Rose. We have to stop her. Let's try the same thing.'

Kaleb thought Rose looked very like the twins, though in old-fashioned clothes. The children tried to make their presence felt to scare her away. She at first seemed puzzled, as if she sensed something, but after stopping for a moment she carried on walking. Rose emerged from the west range corridor and crossed the corridor beneath the north range, apparently intending to unlock a door on its far side. Then she stopped and looked to her right. Kaleb realised she'd noticed the open door to the octagonal cellar. She turned and held up her oil lamp, as if to see better.

'Oh no,' said Florence. 'If she goes over to the open door, she'll meet Edward Murray and we'll have failed.'

'Quiet!' whispered Isobella. 'You said you thought that Lily's voice sounded like mine when we heard her ghost call out in 1887. Let me try something. Turn your torches off.'

Rose seemed undecided what to do. Kaleb watched as Isobella walked over and stood close behind her, now in the light of Rose's oil lamp, then spoke to her in a clear, calm voice.

'Rose, it's Lily. Please listen to me. Please walk over and close that door. Then lock it. The key is still in the lock. Whatever you do, don't look inside the room.'

Rose looked round with a confused expression on her face. She seemed to look right through Isobella.

Isobella spoke again, with more urgency in her voice. 'Rose, it's Lily. You must be quick. This is important. That's right. Keep moving that way. Now just close the door. I know you can hear someone inside but don't look. Be quick! That's right. Now turn the key in the lock and take it out. Yes, you've done it! I love you, Rose, and all your future family will love you too.'

Kaleb felt an intense chill sweep over him and found

himself sitting on a stone floor. He switched his torch on and flicked its light around. He saw Quoia sitting a short distance away. She turned her torch on a moment later.

Kaleb stood up and dusted down the back of his jeans. 'Quoia, we're still in the same place but the house is ruined again. Look, you can see the stars above us and the moonlight shining on some of the walls. He shone his torch at the end of the corridor. And there's the octagonal cellar, only with no door.'

'I think we're back in 2020,' said Quoia. 'But where are Florence and Isobella?'

CHAPTER TWENTY-SEVEN

A feeling of dread swept over Kaleb. 'You don't think they've simply disappeared, do you, Quoia? Did saving Lily and changing their family history really mean they don't exist anymore?'

Quoia sounded close to tears. 'I don't know, Kaleb. I wish I did. I just wish they'd listened to me. Let's see if we can find them. First, though, we need to find out what we can about where we are.'

'We're in "The House With 46 Chimneys",' said Kaleb. 'There you are. I can remember what Isobella and Florence call the house, and I can remember them too. They can't have never existed.'

'We just don't know, Kaleb. And when I said "where", I didn't mean the place.' She took her phone out of her coat pocket. 'My phone's totally dead, like it was after we went through that door in the stables. Hang on. No, I can't get it to switch on. You have a go.'

'Mine's the same.'

'Maybe modern technology doesn't cope well with time travel,' said Quoia. 'I wanted to know the time and date. I'd also hoped to call Florence. For all we know the twins have come back to the right time somewhere else. Perhaps by the steps at the back of the house or in the stables.'

'Why would that have happened?' asked Kaleb.

'I don't know. I suppose I'm just trying to keep alive the hope that they still exist and are back here in 2020.'

'Well let's go and look,' said Kaleb. 'The only way we know of getting out of this level of the house is up the ramp at the back, not far from the stone steps. We can check there. Then we can go to the stables.'

'Is it possible they're even nearer?' asked Quoia. 'Let's shout their names.'

Quoia and Kaleb called out for Florence and Isobella but all they got in return were echoes off the walls of the old ruined house.

Then Kaleb led the way to the back of the building. He paused in the courtyard.

'Look,' he said, pointing above the south range. 'You can see from here that it's a full moon again.'

'I hope that confirms that we are back in 2020,' said Quoia. 'I mean, it's certainly not 1887, is it?' She waved her arms at the ruins around them.

Kaleb led the way past the exit ramp and went to the alcove with the stone steps.

'They're not here,' said Quoia. 'Let's call their names again.'

Again, there was no response.

'I think the stables are the best hope,' said Quoia. 'Hang on. Kaleb, do you feel anything here?'

Kaleb stood still for a moment and thought. 'No, nothing at all. I'm worried about Florence and Isobella, obviously, but I've got no goosebumps and none of the bad feelings I've had here before.'

'It's the same with me,' said Quoia. 'Now it feels just like any other part of the house, even in the dark. Perhaps stopping Lily's death, and Ruby's, has meant this place no longer carries echoes of those tragedies. Look, let's go to the stables. I fear that's our last chance of finding Florence and Isobella.'

The children climbed the ramp from the courtyard to the edge of the wood and picked their way along the path round the outside of the ruined house. Then, on the better track, they headed for the stables at a fast walking pace set by Quoia.

Kaleb felt no sense of anything scary or wrong or out of place as they passed the front corner of the stables. He followed Quoia through the partly opened main doors and the passage and into the overgrown courtyard.

'Come on! Quickly!' Quoia lit her way with the torch.

She stopped in front of the faded yellow door, which stood open, as it had on their previous visits.

'Are you scared?' asked Kaleb.

'No. It feels really odd that I'm not scared. It's totally different, as if there's nothing special here.'

'Me neither,' said Kaleb. 'Let's go in.'

Quoia led the way. To Kaleb the hallway seemed the same as it had earlier. Except for one thing.

'The door to the stables is open,' he said. 'It looks like someone's forced it open from this side.'

'Yes, look at those marks on the door frame. I don't think they were there earlier.' They both walked through the doorway into the stables and shone their torches around.

'It's just a big derelict room,' said Quoia. 'I think there was a ceiling in 1887 and you can see most of that's gone. The floor's rotting away in places too. Look, let's call for Florence and Isobella.'

Again, there was no answer. They went out into the courtyard and called again.

'There's obviously no-one here,' said Quoia.

Kaleb thought she sounded like she was crying. He felt like

he was about to as well.

'Should we get help?' asked Kaleb.

'Even if our phones worked, I'm not sure that dialling 999 would really help. If we tried to explain what has happened, they'd say we were bonkers or just making it up to attract attention.'

'So, let's go and tell Fliss,' said Kaleb. 'She'll know what to do.'

'I don't think anyone will know what to do,' said Quoia. 'But you're right. We should tell her. That means we'll have to find our way through the wood at the back of the house by ourselves and in the dark. I know there's nothing to fear there now, but it would be so easy to get lost.'

'We could go round the wood instead,' said Kaleb. 'Do you remember? On Monday Fliss told us that the track on the far side of the wood comes round it and ends up at the stables. It would be further, but we'd not get lost.'

Perhaps because they'd not taken this route before, the track that followed the edge of the wood seemed much longer. At least the surface was good, and they were able to walk quickly.

After a while Kaleb recognised where they were, approaching the T-junction of tracks formed with the one coming from the main road.

There was, as usual, no traffic on the main road as they approached it.

'Hang on,' said Quoia. 'There's a group of people with torches crossing the road, coming this way. Let's stand off to one side and keep ours off. Though they might have seen us already.'

In the light from the full moon and the faint backlight of a streetlight in the village, Kaleb watched as six figures approached along the track.

'Quoia,' he said quietly, 'I think the two in front are Florence and Isobella. Fliss and Jude and Jamie are with them, and a man.'

'Florence! Isobella!' screamed Quoia. 'We thought you'd been lost.'

'Quoia! Kaleb! We were coming to look for you. Where have you been?'

The four children embraced in the centre of the path.

'Hang on everyone,' said Fliss. 'It seems we're all safely accounted for. Should we go back to Forthview House, preferably in twos so as not to alarm any villagers still not in their beds? We can then talk about what's happened tonight. I've already heard a really odd story from Florence and Isobella and I think perhaps we need to talk before we go to bed. I was wondering how we might do that while preserving social distancing but having seen the four of you hugging each other I suspect there's no point.'

Kaleb and Quoia were first back at the house.

'There's a white van on the drive, next to Fliss's car,' said Kaleb. 'I think it might be the one that the gardener, Andrew, was driving on Monday.'

'I wondered who the man with Fliss was,' said Quoia. 'It seems strange that Andrew is here.'

After they'd let themselves in with the front door key Jude had given them, Quoia and Kaleb left the door unlocked and went up to the kitchen, as instructed by Fliss. Isobella and Florence were next to arrive and the four embraced again. Then Jude and Jamie came up the stairs.

'This is really cool!' said Jamie.

Kaleb realised Jamie had never seen the inside of Forthview House before, only its garden.

'We looked for you everywhere,' said Isobella. 'After Rose had locked the door to the wine cellar, we felt that strange chill again and she disappeared into thin air, right in front of us. But the two of you disappeared too.'

Florence continued. 'We went out the back door and came round the side of the house, to find it was a full moon again, and completely dark. That meant we were back in 1887. We decided the most likely place to find you was in the stables. When we got there, it was deserted except for Peter Simmonds, who we found talking to Sultan again. The horse seemed calm and happy. It was as if we were being shown, just Isobella and me, that we'd broken the historical chain and that Lily, Ruby and Peter had been saved.'

'Then we felt that chill again,' said Isobella. 'Only this time it wasn't just a passing thing, it persisted. Peter and Sultan disappeared but the stables seemed to be frozen in a sort of transition between 1887 and 2020. You could see both, the stable and the ruin, sort of blending into one another. We couldn't get out through the larger door, so we tried the one at the other end, the one from the hallway behind the yellow door. That was also solid and immovable. That was when Jamie and Jude helped us.'

'Jamie and I were in the hallway,' said Jude. 'We heard banging and then Florence and Isobella's voices from behind the door. Jamie found a piece of metal on the ground outside and by working together we forced the door open. Isobella and Florence came out shivering. It was like they'd been in a freezer.'

'Wait,' said Quoia. 'What were you doing there?'

'I think Andrew's van has just driven off towards the village,' said Kaleb, who had been standing by the windows at the front of the lounge.

'Yes, but can we focus on this for a minute, Kaleb? Jude, what were you and Jamie doing in the ruined stables in the middle of the night?'

'We were following you,' said Jude. 'We wanted to know why you'd all gone off without telling us. Jamie heard his sisters leave the cottage and texted me. I checked and found you and Kaleb had gone too. Jamie and I met up on the green and were able to keep you four in sight. It was difficult in the woods behind the house because we were making too much noise. I think you saw us there and again in the basement of the house. But you didn't realise it was us, so we were able to follow you to the stables.'

'The four of you went through that yellow door in the corner of the courtyard,' said Jamie. 'Then you disappeared. We went in but you weren't there. The door on the side wouldn't move, and there was obviously nothing up the stairs to the upper floor.'

Jude picked up the story again. 'We were trying to work out what to do when we heard Isobella and Florence.'

'How long after we all disappeared did you get the door open and let Florence and Isobella out?' asked Quoia.

'I don't know,' said Jude. 'A few minutes at the most.'

'Once we got out, the four of us started looking for you two,' said Florence. 'We searched the stables, obviously, and then went to the house. We looked in the wine cellars and went to the end of the north range, where the steps are. You weren't anywhere.'

'We didn't know what else to do,' said Isobella, 'so we came to tell Fliss you were missing. When we arrived, she was on the drive, moving stuff out of the garage and into a white van. She said the van belonged to her gardener, Andrew, who was helping her. He seemed nice and when we told her what had happened, we all set off to find you. You know the rest.'

'How much of the story did you tell her?' asked Quoia.

'Only a summary. We were all standing on the drive in the glare of the security light. We just told her enough about what had happened to get her to agree to help look for you. Andrew offered to help too.'

'How long do you think it was between Jude and Jamie breaking down the door and you meeting us on the track?' asked Quoia.

'I don't know,' said Isobella. 'Our phones have died so there's no way to tell the time. I just wasn't paying attention. Why?'

'It seems really odd that you were looking for us at the same time as we were looking for you, and in the same places, and yet we didn't meet until we did.'

'What do you mean?' asked Florence.

Quoia told them what had happened to her and Kaleb between Rose's disappearance and the meeting on the track.

'Could it be that our times were different?' asked Isobella.

'What do you mean?' asked Quoia.

'We know from Jamie and Jude that Florence and I came back out of the stable a short time after going into it. That meant we'd come back to the present at almost the same time as we'd left it, even though we did lots in between those two things happening. But we also came back to the present in the same place as we went back to the past.'

'I know what you're going to say,' said Kaleb. 'You think that because Quoia and I came back to the present in a different place to where we went into the past, then time might have worked differently for us.'

'Yes, Kaleb. If your return to the present took account of the time that you'd personally seen pass in 1887 and in 1828, then you might have returned to 2020 significantly later than Florence and I did. If so, then you searched the same places for us that we did for you, but you did it later than we did. When you were searching, we'd already given up and had come back here to fetch Fliss.'

'That would make as much sense as anything else that's happened tonight,' said Quoia. 'Hang on, here's Fliss.'

CHAPTER TWENTY-EIGHT

Fliss came up the stairs into the kitchen, followed by Erica Durand, who looked like she'd just got out of bed.

'Right, first things first,' said Fliss. 'I'll get cocoa for everyone. It's extremely late and I think it might be rather later before any of us get back to our beds. Erica's here because I thought she would want to hear what's been going on. Given what Florence and Isobella told me a little earlier, this concerns her as much as anyone in the room.'

With the cocoa made and the mugs on the table, and with enough seats pulled through from the studio to the kitchen, Fliss looked round at them. 'Right, I think we need the full story, however long it takes. Who wants to start?'

In the end, it was Isobella and Quoia who did most of the talking, with help from Florence and Kaleb and a little from Jude and Jamie. Fliss asked questions occasionally but Erica Durand said nothing. Kaleb didn't think that her gaze had shifted from the cocoa mug she was holding on the table in front of her. She seemed content to listen and let her cocoa go cold.

There was a silence after the different parts of the story had been told.

It was Fliss who broke it. 'What you are saying is that you went back to 1887, and then to 1828, to put something right that you think has blighted your family ever since?'

Florence and Isobella nodded.

'And it sounds like you succeeded, because whatever presence there was at the back of the house and in the stables seems to have disappeared?'

Quoia and Kaleb nodded.

'Well I must say I've never heard anything like it. I'm not sure there's much more I can usefully add except that I'm so pleased you are all here and able to talk about it. I can't pretend to understand what lies behind some of what you experienced but it does all seem to have worked out for the best, despite the risks you took. Let's just be grateful that Quoia's butterfly effect didn't have the feared consequences, for whatever reason. What do you think, Erica?'

Kaleb was surprised to see tears streaming down Erica Durand's face when she looked up.

'What I want to say most is how sorry I am that the two of you, Florence and Isobella, had to go through this experience. I'm sorry to everyone else who got caught up in it too. When my mother, Lily, tried to tell me about Lily Robertson and Ruby Simmonds and the ghost and everything else, I refused to listen. What she didn't know was that my grandmother, Mary, had already told me all about it.

'I hoped, to be honest, that the story would die with me. That was why I asked my mother not to tell you girls about it, though I'm not surprised to hear that she did.'

'Grandma Lily said you'd laughed off the story when she tried to tell you,' said Isobella.

'That seemed the best way to make it seem less important. After I heard the story something about it always troubled me. I'd lived with my mother and gran and two older brothers at the cottage since I was quite small, after my father had died. We'd often been to the old house but something about the place always really unsettled me. After I heard the story from Grandma Mary, I never went there again.'

'But you never stopped us going,' said Isobella.

'No, I thought if I tried to do that, it would just make the house seem more attractive in your mind and you'd be more likely to go anyway. That didn't work very well either, did it?'

Erica took a drink of her cocoa, which Kaleb thought must be completely cold by now.

'In the end, I moved away. I went to university. I got a good job in London. And I got married to your father. It all came back to me, though, when I had twin daughters in 2006. Given what had happened to two previous sets of female twins in my family, it truly terrified me when you two came along.

'Then things went wrong between your father and me. In 2014, I was left with no choice. I did what women in my family have had to do too often over the past 130 or so years. I moved back to the cottage with my children, always dreading what seemed to me to be less a family story than a family curse. Believe me that if I'd had any other choice, including moving to Timbuktu, I'd have taken it. I've been frightened of something like this happening ever since.'

'Well it has now, Mum,' said Florence, 'and we're both all right. We're fine.'

'Yes, I'd like to thank you, Quoia and Kaleb, for standing by my daughters and helping them through what you all experienced. And I'd like to thank Jude and Jamie for being there to get that door open when that was needed. Now, if that clock's right we're all up long past our bedtimes. I think we'd better be getting home.'

After Erica and the Durand children had left, Fliss locked the front door behind them and came back up to the kitchen.

'I think we need to be heading for our beds, too.'

'Fliss,' said Quoia, 'why was Andrew here tonight? The twins saw you moving stuff from the garage into his van when they and the boys arrived.'

'I said I'd tell you on Thursday. I will keep that promise.'

Quoia pointed at the clock. 'It's Thursday now.'

'I'm sure you must be too tired for more talking,' said Fliss.

'I'm not,' said Quoia.

'Nor me,' said Jude.

Kaleb just smiled when Fliss looked at him.

She smiled back. 'All right then. But I would like you to promise you'll not tell anyone else what I'm about to tell you.'

The children all promised.

'OK, then. Let me get more cocoa first.'

'I'm sure we can manage without,' said Quoia.

'Perhaps, but I can't,' said Fliss, 'and you are all welcome to join me. Put all the dirty dishes over by the sink. We can sort them out in the morning.'

'Do we need to be careful picking up stuff the Durands handled?' asked Jude.

'I think that from now on the only way we're going to come anywhere near to obeying the rules is if we consider the Durands and ourselves to be a single household,' said Fliss. 'I understand the hugging when you met up again this evening, and the hand-holding earlier was obviously necessary. But it does make a mockery of social distancing.'

After she sat down again, Fliss took a sip of her cocoa.

'It's like you said earlier,' said Quoia, 'who wants to start? Only this time I think it has to be you, Fliss.'

Fliss smiled. 'Very well then. I think I told you that when we lived in Stirling both your Uncle Jim and I were smokers. What I didn't tell you was that once the children had gone to university, we occasionally used to smoke things that weren't legal. I mean marijuana. We had a nice garden there and plenty of space and a big shed, and once Belinda and David were no longer spending vacations with us, we started growing and preparing our own in the shed.

'That continued after we moved here, though here we used the garage. Then Jim died and I stopped smoking, both tobacco and marijuana. The problem was that marijuana isn't just something that's smoked recreationally. There are people who believe it has medicinal qualities too. While living in Stirling I'd started to supply three or four friends with marijuana for medicinal purposes. I didn't make money out of it, but I knew that what I was doing was completely illegal despite that. If I'm honest, I knew what I was doing wasn't just illegal, it was also wrong. I just carried on doing it because I was able to convince myself I was doing it for good reasons.

'Then Belinda came to stay last Christmas. As Andrew was also staying, Belinda used the apartment over the garage. One day, Boxing Day it was, she noticed a funny smell coming from the door leading to the garage at the foot of the stairs up to the apartment. As the key to that door was on the same ring as the one for the apartment, she went in. To say she was angry about what she found would be an understatement. She told me that if I carried on, she'd never have anything to do with me again. Then she got in her car and left, even though she'd been planning to stay over Hogmanay too.

'I should say that I'd also been getting similar pressure, though much more gently, from Andrew. I think I've told you that he was our gardener in Stirling and has gardened here from when we moved in. He knew what Jim and I were doing and what I've been doing since Jim died. He never had anything to do with it himself and he never approved.

'After Belinda went ballistic and left, Andrew suggested that I should agree to wind down what I was doing by a set date, which would give the people relying on me a chance to find alternative sources. I contacted Belinda and told her that I'd have stopped completely and permanently by the time I was due to go to Vancouver next month. I'd never get anyone to look after it for three weeks in my absence anyway. Andrew's the only one I'd trust, and he'd never go near it.'

'So that was why you had to go and see someone in Stirling to deliver a painting that never existed?' asked Quoia.

'That's right.'

'And why you took paints they didn't need to a friend in Greenock?'

'That's right, too.'

'But what about John MacDonald?'

'Ah, yes. I mentioned he had a wife and two children. One of them has a condition that some people believe can be helped by medicinal marijuana. He's been the one who has been most concerned since I told people I'd be stopping. I believe the lockdown has made it particularly difficult for him to find alternative sources.

'What I took over to Greenock was pretty much everything I had left, and that wasn't much. John had been texting me and wasn't happy that I didn't have any for him. I simply stopped answering his texts and then his calls. That was why he came over last night, Tuesday night. I feel sorry for him, but I can't risk losing Belinda.'

'And why was Andrew here tonight?' asked Quoia.

'He's been really pleased I've been ending this,' said Fliss. 'After my row with Belinda, Andrew told me that he could never have formed a long-term relationship with me if that made him party to growing and supplying drugs. My problem has been getting rid of some quite specialised equipment that I've used to grow and process the stuff. Lamps and other things.

'I phoned Andrew this morning and told him about the visit by John MacDonald. We agreed I needed to get rid of anything still left in the garage as quickly as possible. Andrew's brother is a fisherman who sails out of Pittenweem in Fife. Andrew offered to pick up the equipment I had in the garage and take it to Pittenweem. Then he and his brother would sail out and dump it at sea. He'll be well on his way to Fife now. I only hope he's not stopped by the police.'

'Does that mean that there's nothing left in the garage to show what you've been doing?' asked Quoia.

'I'm sure if a police forensics team turned up, they'd have no problem finding traces of marijuana. But that will fade over time and if you walked into the garage, you'd see nothing suspicious. If you like I'll show you all, but it really should wait until the morning given how late it is. And I should warn you that I wasn't lying when I said I was embarrassed by how much of a mess the rest of the garage is.'

'Perhaps we can help you sort it out now,' said Quoia.

CHAPTER TWENTY-NINE

SATURDAY THE 18TH OF APRIL 2020

Saturday dawned cloudy and cool. Not that they could complain, thought Kaleb. The weather since their adventure at 'The House With 46 Chimneys' had been generally good. In the week and a half since then, he'd not noticed any rain. Come to think of it, he'd not noticed any since they had come to stay with Fliss, two and a half weeks earlier.

Life had become very routine. They'd done schoolwork most mornings, then art. They'd gone for walks most afternoons. They had also helped Fliss sort things out in the garage, though with the council recycling centres closed during the lockdown, there were now a lot of full black plastic bags piled up on one side of it.

It had taken Kaleb and Quoia's phones two days to start working again, which had been a relief to them. Explaining to Mummy and Daddy why they needed new phones might not have been easy.

On the Thursday, the day after Kaleb had thought Florence and Isobella had been lost for good, they'd been to visit Dunmore Park with Fliss and the Durand children, their mother and Oban. All the nasty feelings had disappeared, for him, for Quoia, for Erica Durand and, it seemed, for Oban.

Since then, they'd seen a lot of the Durands. It had become clear that Jude really liked Isobella. Much more than she seemed to like Jude, Kaleb thought.

The two families had been careful about how they saw one another. The Durands would always come to Forthview House singly or in pairs, and always go into the garden before entering the house from the back.

Andrew had also called round a few times. Kaleb liked him and hoped that he and Fliss would make each other happy. Fliss had told the children that Andrew's drive to Pittenweem had been a tense one, but he'd got there without being stopped.

Today, though, was going to be far from routine and Kaleb was looking forward to it. It would be the first time he'd seen his parents in two and a half weeks.

Their father had been out of hospital for a week and was now able to drive the small automatic car he'd been loaned to replace his written-off Mercedes estate. He was planning to return to work on Monday. Fliss had told the children that their mother was strongly against this and wanted him to take much longer off work. That way, he could look after the children in Kirkliston. He felt he had to do what he could at the hospital. He couldn't work as a surgeon with one arm still in plaster and a sling, but he wanted to do whatever he could to help his colleagues who were under huge pressure because of the virus.

Fliss and Henry had planned the visit carefully.

The children's father had rung when their mother, who was driving, was coming through Airth.

The children stood with Fliss in front of the garage, beside her car.

Their mother stopped the car at the bottom of the drive and both she and their father got out, both looking upset. Kaleb guessed they'd been arguing on the way.

There was some awkward small talk. Kaleb desperately

233

wanted to run and give his mother a hug, and his father. He knew he couldn't. He knew they wanted to give the three children hugs but couldn't.

'Well this is what we're officially here for,' said Mummy with an awkward smile. 'If anyone asks, we're delivering shopping.' She walked forwards a few paces and placed a plastic shopping bag on the ground. 'Bread flour and yeast. It's like gold dust around us too, but the man who runs the village shop came up with the goods.'

Kaleb saw she had tears in her eyes as she continued. 'I do wish we could all be together again.'

'We do too, Mummy,' said Quoia.

'I'm so grateful to you Fliss, for keeping our darlings safe for us in this strange world we all now live in.'

'We both are,' said Daddy.

Kaleb thought it was as well that Mummy and Daddy didn't know too much about what the children had been doing while staying with Fliss.

They spent a little longer talking about things that didn't really matter, separated by more than just two metres of Fliss's drive.

Then it seemed to Kaleb that they all just ran out of things to say. After everyone told everyone else that they loved them, Mummy and Daddy got back into her car and she reversed from the lane onto the drive before pulling away in the direction of the village. The children waved as they went. Mummy waved out of her window. Kaleb realised that Daddy couldn't wave out of his.

All three children were crying after the car had disappeared from view.

'I'm sorry, children,' said Fliss. 'I know how much you want to be together again as a proper family.'

'I'd love to go home with Mummy and Daddy and I really look forward to doing that when we can,' said Jude. 'But in the meantime, we're at home here with you, Fliss.' He gave her a hug.

All four of them were crying when they went back into the house.

AUTHOR'S NOTE

This book is a work of fiction and should be read as such. All characters are fictional and, except as noted below, any resemblances to real people, either living or dead, are purely coincidental.

Likewise, the events that are described in this book are the products of the author's imagination.

The only real people mentioned in this book are the 19th Century Earls of Dunmore, the Murray family. They built Dunmore Park, and the Pineapple, and the village of Dunmore. Their murderous cousin, Edward Murray, is an invention.

Most of the places that appear in this book are real. These includes Dunmore Park, whose ruins can be seen on aerial photos to have 46 chimneys, as well as The Pineapple, Elphinstone Tower, the stable block, and the village of Dunmore.

Places visited incidentally are also real, including Tappoch Broch, Torwood Castle, Torwood Blue Pool, the Antonine Wall and Rough Castle. Not forgetting Sainsbury's in Stirling, of course.

Forthview House is an invention. Its site occupies part of what in the real world is a farmer's field beside the River Forth. The design of the house is based on one whose build was featured on a TV programme and which is located on the other side of the River Forth quite some distance downstream.

The real locations are generally as they are described in this book. I say 'generally' because of the elephant in the room.

This is a book about people coping during the lockdown that was imposed in late March 2020 to contain and control the coronavirus pandemic. It depicts one family's life in the early stages of lockdown, and it was written during the lockdown. The characters in the book break the lockdown rules frequently, in small ways and in larger ones. This proved necessary simply to make them interesting enough to write about and, I hope, to read about.

Their creator did a rather better job of obeying the rules. That meant I had to abandon my normal approach of visiting and photographing every inch of every real location I use in my novels. In describing places, I had to rely on photographs taken on earlier visits made for other purposes and memories of those visits, backed up by Google Earth and Street View. As a result, some details are inevitably not right.

During the editing of this book, after the initial lockdown was eased, I revisited the main locations used to see how accurately I had described them. I have, however, resisted the temptation to make any changes to my descriptions of them. To my mind there's a fitting sense of circularity in writing a book about the strange world we found ourselves in during lockdown that has itself been entirely constrained by that same strange world.

Moving on, I want to thank my wonderful wife Maureen, whose company made lockdown bearable and whose comments and advice as this book evolved from the germ of an idea to a finished story have been hugely helpful.

I would also like to thank my grandson, Alistair who, as noted in the dedication, helped me write this book. The comments and suggestions he made via text exchanges helped me see the lockdown through the eyes of a 10-year-old. He also helped keep me grounded – unlike four of the characters – firmly in the right century. The character of Kaleb is inspired by Alistair.